Roxy's Song

LOVE IN LITTLE RIVER | BOOK ONE

RANEE S. CLARK

SWEETLY US

Cover design by Sweetly Us Press

Cover Photo Credit: "Journey" Impact Photography | Adobe Stock

Editor: Jenny Proctor | www.jennyproctor.com

Published by Sweetly Us Press

www.sweetlyuspress.com

OTHER WORKS BY RANEÉ S. CLARK

Playing for Keeps
Double Play
Love, Jane
Meant for You

Beneath the Bellemont Sky

CHAPTER ONE

R oxy Adams studied the poster that took up nearly the entire front window of the Little River Mercantile and sighed.

"I'm sure you're as excited as anyone to see Tag's concert," Mrs. Davis said as she glanced over at the picture and then started pulling Roxy's purchases over the scanner.

Roxy forced a smile and forced herself not to take another look at the six-foot-tall poster with the handsome, blond-haired man in a ball cap, a guitar slung across his back and his head tipped to the sky as he crooned into a microphone.

"Of course," she said, since that's what Mrs. Davis expected. And if it were Tag Turner singing on Friday night, she might be. But it was Taggart Dubois, an unarguable star of country music. Not the boy who used to sing his soul to her on occasion.

The truth was, she wasn't even going. Among every other person in the county, her former friend was unlikely to notice she wasn't in the sold-out audience.

"My, I don't know how long it's been since that boy came home," Mrs. Davis went on, packing the last of Roxy's items away in the fabric bag Roxy had brought in. The woman was very efficient at her job.

Eight years. Since he graduated and left town, hitchhiking his way across the country to Nashville and stardom. "Mmm," she said out loud. She swiped her card and waved goodbye, echoing Mrs. Davis's admonition to have a nice day.

She didn't even take a second look at the poster as she headed out to her truck in the parking lot.

The drive back to the Arrow C was quiet. The local radio station had been playing Tag's hits non-stop the last week in preparation for his appearance at the county fair that weekend. Normally Roxy didn't mind hearing a song or two—or switching stations when she just didn't want to listen—but the last few days it had just been easier to keep it off. And by the time she remembered she didn't want to listen to the radio, she was already driving and couldn't switch on the playlist from her phone.

She pulled into her garage and paused a minute to take a deep breath. The local motels in town were booked, thanks to the concert, so the guests at the ranch this weekend were only interested in the rooms the Arrow C had available, not the many dude ranch entertainments they provided. Roxy's great-grandmother Rozzy Adams would have been sad to see Roxy move out of the big, Victorian ranch-house-slash-mansion that had been the home of the Nikels-Pender-Adams clan for seven generations. But Roxy thanked the heavens, especially this weekend, for her own space in the newer house she'd built behind it—renovating the turn-of-the-century brick mansion solely into rooms for those who came to experience a slice of western life. She wouldn't have to run into one of the many concert goers staying at the Ranch House—the simple name she'd chosen for it— and then end up pretending excitement for an event she'd dreaded since it was first announced.

As she stepped into the kitchen and set the bag of groceries on the counter, readying to put them away, she heard gravel crunching in the drive. Looking through the open kitchen and living room space to the big picture window in the front, she saw Nash Roberts hop out of his Jeep and head up the wide, wooden steps to her front door. He knocked quickly, already stepping inside as she called for him to come in. In the seven months since they'd started dating, he'd become comfortable in her home. She stowed away the milk and eggs in the fridge before heading into the living room to greet him.

Nash waved an envelope around before dipping down to kiss her hello, then gently tapped the edge of it on her nose. "Guess what I won today, Miss Adams."

Roxy's heart sank. Despite not listening to the radio for several days, she did know that the station was giving away at least a dozen tickets to Tag's concert. She plastered on a smile anyway.

"You probably could've gotten us these," Nash went on, his grin stretching wider and wider. "But I got backstage passes! And tickets!" He whooped and spun her around before setting her back down and pulling her close to kiss her again.

Roxy tried to lose herself in the way he wrapped his arms around her back and the softness of his lips, but her brain kept spinning around having to go to Tag's concert. Having to see him up close for the first time since her freshman year of college, when he showed up at her dorm on the brink of stardom and begged her to come along. Since she called him crazy for thinking he actually loved her and that it wasn't just years of friendship speaking. Since he'd claimed she'd broken his heart in half.

"You know I haven't spoken to Tag in forever," she murmured.

Nash scoffed, but still grinned. "Tag Turner would drop his guitar and run whenever Roxy called," he teased.

"Maybe Tag Turner would." She slapped Nash's shoulder. He was a few years older than her and Tag and knew all about their friendship in high school. It might be annoying at the moment that he knew all about her past, but she loved him for being able to give her something Tag would have never been able too—a home. An actual home in one spot; namely, Little River. The town she'd grown up in, along with generations of her ancestors. A town she helped support with the tourists her bed and breakfast brought in.

Nash turned serious, pulling Roxy back to him and leaning over her. "You're right. You haven't talked to him in forever, and it's about time you did, Rox."

She shook her head and nudged away from him, heading back to the kitchen to put away the rest of her groceries. "Tag is not coming back to Little River to reconnect with anyone. He's coming back because that's what rock stars like him do—show up in their hometown to impress everyone and then move back on." *Like he always does,* she added to herself, careful not to slam the cupboard shut when she put away the bread. She'd been right to turn him down when he asked her to give up everything and go on the road with him. He'd forgotten all about her the minute she said no. And if she'd said yes? How long before he would have forgotten about her anyway? Just like in high school, there was always a swarm of girls who fell under the sway of that silly spell his singing put over everyone. He never needed Roxy.

Nash leaned over the island and snagged her hand as she moved to put away the fruit. He threaded his fingers through hers. "Then go and be impressed along with everyone else. There's nothing wrong with showing Tag he did well for himself. It doesn't make you wrong for not following him like he wanted if you tell him good job."

She paused. "I know. I'm sorry for not being more excited. It'll be a fun night and I'm happy for you." She edged around the island and put her arms around him. "But then, I've always known you were lucky. You got me."

"Boy, am I, honey."

And this time Roxy did succeed in losing herself in Nash's kiss.

ROXY DISCOVERED she would also have to swear off social media, probably until weeks after Tag's concert. Even her own sister had joined in the hullabaloo, posting a picture of her, Tag, and Roxy (and tagging Roxy, which was how she ended up not scrolling right past it) from high school. *We sure are proud of you, Tag,* Taylor had written. *Wish I was home with everyone to cheer you on Friday night!*

Maybe Nash wouldn't mind if Taylor took Roxy's ticket.

Swearing off social media was easy. If only she could swear off the Ranch House, like her mother did most of the year. Even after Roxy had renovated it, her mother saw her father around every corner. The same way Roxy never could quite escape the fact that Tag had spent far too much time in this home during their growing up years. Roxy's mother, Anna, lived in Arizona full time now, and Roxy always went for a few weeks in the winter when Wyoming became unbearable and she could swear it would never get warm again. Not many guests braved staying at the Ranch House in mid-January.

Unfortunately, the manager, Bellamy, texted that morning that she needed Roxy to come sign some paperwork. Bellamy took care of much of the day-to-day business these days, leaving Roxy to the big picture management of the ranch and the Ranch House. Lately she'd been spending a lot of time researching various projects she could introduce on the ranch to give back. The Ranch House had revived the flagging tourist trade when they'd opened a couple years before, but Roxy knew there was more she could do for her beloved community.

Though various things had trimmed the size of the ranch in recent years, the Arrow C was still one of the biggest ranches in Wyoming, and Roxy had been trying to find a way to harness its success for the good of the county and the state. She'd already planned a summer retreat for some low-income kids from Casper to come spend a week on the ranch later in the summer, but the thought that she should do something bigger to contribute kept nagging at her.

When she walked in the front door of the Ranch House, she made sure to put on a smile for the guests milling around. The once sixteen-room mansion now boasted fifteen guest rooms that made it the perfect hideaway, and every single one of those rooms was at max capacity this weekend. Roxy had been pleased to hire a couple of high school kids from in town to help with the extra load.

"Miss Adams?" A teenage girl broke away from where she sat with her family at the dining room table eating the buffet breakfast that the staff had set out.

"Yes?" Roxy steeled herself for some question concerning Tag. Bellamy had insisted on putting a big picture on the website for the Ranch House of Tag and Roxy out on a ride on Arrow C land—*The*

Arrow C Ranch House is proud to welcome home Taggart Dubois to Little River! Roxy rolled her eyes every time she saw it.

"Is it true that you knew Taggart Dubois growing up?" she asked.

It was painful to keep her smile from turning sad or bitter. "Sure is." Roxy nodded toward the kitchen. "He sat at this very table more often than I can count." That was a stretch. He'd sat at the dining room table that had been in this one's place. That old one had seen too many dinners with Tag Turner, too many games of spoons, too many late-night conversations with all their friends to be presentable in an establishment like the Ranch House.

The girl gave a soft *squee* and used her phone to snap a selfie of herself in front of the table. Her fingers moved rapidly over the keyboard of her phone and Roxy was, thankfully, forgotten. She slipped away to Bellamy's office. It had been Roxy's mother's office before she'd moved and left the house to Roxy.

When Roxy opened one of the pretty French doors that closed off the space from the rest of the living area, Bellamy sat behind a rustic wooden desk, intent on the computer in front of her. She looked up when Roxy closed the door behind her. "Good morning."

"What have you got?" Roxy settled into one of the arm chairs across from the desk. The decorator had given the room the same homey feel as the rest of the house, and if it hadn't been for the big desk, it might have felt like a sitting room instead.

Bellamy pushed some papers across the desk along with a pen. "License renewals," she explained. Then she handed Roxy a sticky note. "Danny said Four Star called again," Bellamy said, referring to the ranch foreman.

Roxy shook her head as soon as she heard the energy company's name. "The answer is still no."

Bellamy nodded and steepled her hands. "I understand you don't want them mining on the ranch, but you've been wanting to give back, and you should at least consider what something like this would do for the local economy. Year-round jobs, rather than seasonal work to serve the guests we bring out."

Roxy blew out a breath. "I know, I know. I'll give it some more thought but tell Danny to hold them off. We're not deciding anything in a rush."

Bellamy nodded and Roxy set to work signing the paperwork. "It's busy out there," Roxy murmured as she pulled another page forward.

"Best business we've done all summer," Bellamy said proudly. "Thank you, Taggart Dubois."

"Hmph." Roxy signed another paper and handed it over. Bellamy simply grinned.

"Savannah called to make sure we were still good for her wedding this fall, and could she at least please pay the deposit fee? It would make her feel better." Bellamy ticked something off in her notebook as she spoke.

"Absolutely it's still on, and absolutely she will not pay a dime. She's my cousin and my dad would roll over in his grave if a descendent of Big Ed Pender had to pay to get married on her own family's legacy." Roxy laughed. "Besides, she's paying Brook enough for the pictures, that it will be nice advertising when they tell everyone where they held the ceremony. Doing more weddings out here would be good for the town." She ticked off a list of people whose businesses would flourish if they could make the Ranch House a premier event spot. Catering, photography, rentals, entertainment. Between her and Bellamy, they could sweet talk plenty of people into using local businesses, rather than hiring out of Casper or Billings.

She slid the last piece of paperwork over to Bellamy. "Mind if I crawl out your window? Someone out there is on the verge of asking me all of Tag's favorites."

Bellamy arched her brows in an expression with a serious lack of sympathy. "You should quit overthinking it and get into the whole thing. You'd have a lot more fun."

"So that's a no, I can't crawl out your window?"

Bellamy shook her head. "So you told him no ten years ago—"

"Eight," Roxy corrected with an indignant scowl. She wasn't that old yet.

"And he took it bad and didn't talk to you after that. Do you really think it's bugging him as much as it bugs you? I'm sorry to be the one to say it, but he probably forgot about it a long time ago and ignoring every reference to the man isn't hurting him a bit."

Roxy huffed. "When you put it that way, it sounds really childish."

"If the shoe fits, honey," Bellamy murmured, going back to something on the computer.

Roxy huffed again, but Bellamy only laughed and didn't look up as Roxy left the office. Ignoring her friend's insensitivity, she headed out to the main area to brave the fans. They would all be gone by Saturday morning. She could last that long.

CHAPTER TWO

When Nash had showed Roxy those tickets, she hadn't even glanced at where the seats were, but as he kept leading her closer and closer to the stage, her eyes got wider and wider. This close, Tag would be able to look right down and see them, she was sure of it. Or maybe all the lights the crew had brought in to surround the stage would blind him, and she'd be lost in a sea of blackness.

She didn't know. She'd never been to one of Tag's concerts before. Not even before that stupid night in Laramie, back when they were still talking. He'd asked her plenty of times to come and listen to him. To show her around backstage and meet the big names he was opening for at the time. After Laramie, she didn't go to his concerts. She didn't buy his songs. Nash didn't know the half of the lengths she'd gone to prove to Tag Turner that she didn't need him or his fame.

"Wow, Nash!" she had to shout over the rumble of the crowd around them. The thousands of people packed onto the fairgrounds had likely tripled the population of the county for the night.

He turned to look at the stage, cranking his head back to see the crew rushing around with last-minute preparations. "Wow is right. I didn't even realize," he called back to her. He wrapped an arm around her shoulder, pulling her close in the crush of people.

They waved at a group of the guests at the ranch who passed them to get to still-closer seats and then stopped to talk to various people they knew from Little River, several of whom shook Nash's hand vigorously and congratulated him on the great seats and the backstage passes.

"Make sure you say hi to Tag for us, Roxy," too many said. "Tell him how proud we are."

She kept on smiling and nodded that of course she would. If she saw him. If she hadn't yet figured out how to get out of going back-stage with Nash. Nausea? She was already feeling a little sick to her stomach over having to listen to a dozen songs he'd always sworn she'd inspired. Had he moved on from that yet? Just a few months ago, when he'd released his latest hit, she'd accidentally heard some lyrics about walking hand in hand down the middle of the football field. Yeah, that was her.

Her nerves eased up during the opening acts, a couple local bands chosen to represent Little River. She sang along with the crowd around her and grinned during one slower song when Nash pulled her into his arms to sway in the small space allotted them. She leaned against his shoulder and closed her eyes. She could do this. Just hold onto Nash and not think about how it would feel to hear those songs again. They were just songs. Just words. It had been so long since she'd seen Tag. The way those songs had made her ache and made her heart pinch after he walked away had to have faded by now.

The crowd hushed for a moment. Lights swung around them and the cheering started slow, then exploded into a boom when Tag strode onto the stage. Two steps across and the music started. He clapped his hands with the crowd, slowing it to a beat that the people around her changed their frenzied clapping to match.

"I KISSED TAG'S DATE AT HOMECOMING!" a voice shouted from somewhere behind her. Kolby Hunter. Junior year, Roxy had told Tag not to take Macie—that she and Kolby were going to get back together.

On stage, Tag chuckled, along with the crowd around him. "I see you somehow managed to convince that girl to marry you."

Roxy couldn't help smiling. She turned to where Tag was gazing out in the crowd, laughing along with everyone as Kolby leaned over to kiss his wife. Whistles echoed around them, and Roxy couldn't deny the energy building. The pride in the people around her that this boy had been theirs.

"It's good to be home, Little River!" Tag shouted, drawing out the syllables of the town's name. The cheering exploded again, incoherent shouts joining the chorus, and Tag launched into his first song, his most popular. She knew enough to know that it had sat at number one for weeks and was still played constantly on the radio. She'd had to turn it off enough times to know. She'd never listened to all the lyrics before, but the words about home, trucks, farms, and family twisted at her heart. He sang in a nostalgic way, like he'd missed out on something.

He had. But it had been his choice.

Three songs in, the tempo slowed. The band dropped off, and Tag moved center stage, just him and his guitar. It had been so long since she'd heard this particular song it took her a few measures to recognize it. And then she just hoped that it only sounded similar.

But no, the lyrics churned her up even worse. She went still, in shock that he'd sing *this song* at a concert in Little River. This song had not been on any album he'd ever made in the last eight years.

There's a place.
Where everyone's at the game on Friday night.
Where you wave you hand at whoever's driving by
And it's all just right.
There's a house.
Where my mama raised four kids on God and faith
Where the backyard was a stage,
And the kitchen table the place we learned to pray

"Rox?" Nash had leaned over and whispered in her ear. She didn't realize he had his arm around her, holding her close again, swaying softly with her. "What's wrong?"

She turned to see him studying her and she realized how much tension she held in her shoulders, how she clenched her hands so hard, the nails bit into her palms. She softened her knees to sway along and shook her head. "Nothing," she said back.

"There's a girl," she mouthed along to the next words, still not believing that she stood in the middle of thousands of people listening to him say this out loud, not sitting on the bed in her dorm room, tears choking her, Tag's voice broken as he sang. His last plea to make her follow his dream with him.

"*She's every broken piece of every memory I never could let go,*" Tag sang. Could she be imagining that he looked right down at her? That their eyes met? That now of all times, he'd picked back up that old habit of looking at only her no matter how many people listened? "*And I wish that she could see, she's still a part of me.*" Roxy covered her ears with her hands, but that couldn't stop the memory from falling down around her along with the notes.

⬤———————————⬤

"*I can't, Tag.*" *She pushed the guitar away and stood from the bed, turning to look out the window at the scattered lights of Laramie. "This is crazy. You're just..." She didn't know what, but him showing up now and insisting he'd loved her all those years? It didn't make sense. He'd never said a word. "Caught up in all of this and you want a piece of home."*

He came to stand behind her, spinning her around so that he circled her in his arms. "I want you. I mean it, Rox. I have always wanted you." He bent his head over hers, the scruff of days on the road stung her skin when he pressed their lips together. He held her hips, pulling her closer, closer, closer. The sharp scent of his new cologne swirled around her. She ran her fingers on the back of his neck, and his arms shifted, wrapping around her back, pulling them into a cocoon of each other. She'd never imagined they could be this way together. Years of teasing, of silly flirting hadn't prepared her for the way her heart leapt at his kiss.

"How am I supposed to believe you when you're throwing it at me all of a sudden," she murmured when they pulled apart. Confusion and fear had

frozen the warmth in her chest from his nearness, from the passion he'd poured into his kiss.

"I've been saying it for years. You just wouldn't listen."

"I can't do it," she had said out loud. She couldn't trust him. He'd left the day after graduation and she hadn't heard from him in the months between then and when he'd showed up at her dorm. And he'd expected her to walk away from her education, her plans to live near her family on the ranch, just because he'd shown up and said he loved her? He'd never said it before. How could a song count? How was she supposed to know that?

"Roxy?" Nash's eyebrows slanted down with concern.

"Nothing." She forced a smile and leaned into him again, trying to ignore the words and Tag's voice. *It's all in my head. These words aren't for me anymore. It's just a song.* He said he'd always told her, and at first, she'd looked for it in his songs. But he sang those same songs to every woman who came to every concert.

"I wrote that song for a very special someone who's in the audience tonight."

Roxy's gaze snapped to the stage. He walked to the edge and looked right down at her. "I miss you like crazy, Roxy." His words held a lilt as he strummed on his guitar.

Faces swung in her direction, some just following Tag's gaze and staring at the general area around her in confusion.

Nash's hand squeezed hers and she glanced up at him. He grinned, but it was tight around his eyes as he stared at Tag. "Too late!" he shouted, making those around him laugh. Making this all a silly joke that didn't mean anything. *Please, let Tag not pursue it.* This was just like Laramie. A big, grand gesture in Tag Turner style.

Roxy snaked her arm around Nash's waist, clinging to him. Nash was home.

Then Tag swung his guitar around on his back and jumped off the stage. Cries of excitement echoed around him as he pushed his way toward her, hopping over the rows of seats. By the third one, the crowd had started to part. Cell phones were raised all around them, pictures snapping, recording video.

"Rox?" Nash said, looking down at her. She shook her head in confusion.

Tag pulled his guitar back around and started playing again as he came down the row toward her, fans eagerly backing out of his way to make sure this show played out exactly as romantically as Tag probably intended.

This time, when he started to sing again, he started with her name.
Roxy, girl...
I'll never be the same without you,
I'm begging you to listen to me now,
I need your love

The lyrics weren't smooth like any of Tag's other songs. They sounded cobbled together, but somehow more heartfelt than anything she'd ever heard him sing. Beside her, Nash tensed. She squeezed his hand back, begging him to stand by her in this onslaught. Anger heated inside her stomach that Tag would throw this at her so publicly, this encore coming years later than she'd expected. But her anger had to war with a piece of her that was caught up in him.

This whole show,
Has stolen a part of my soul
It's taken the pieces of me
I meant for you to hold
And I need you to see
You're everything to me
Roxy please ... please
Don't turn me down.

"You're crazy," she whispered, shaking her head, but there was no way he heard her above the sound of the music still coming from his band on stage and his guitar now directly in front of her.

He strummed a few more chords, staring directly at her before he stopped and reached for her hand. She backed away into Nash.

"*Come home to me and sing along,*" Tag begged her. "*Please sing along...*"

She shook her head, everything roaring inside of her. She turned to Nash. "I need to get out of here. Now."

He gave a sharp nod and pushed through the row behind them, tugging her along with him. When they reached the aisle, she glanced back at Tag just before Nash put an arm protectively around her.

Tag wore the same look he had just before he walked out of her dorm room in Laramie—like she'd taken his guitar and smashed it over his heart.

✺————————✺

NASH DIDN'T TALK as they drove away from the fairgrounds. The music had started back up before they'd even finished their escape, echoing in the wind that swirled around them as the Jeep sped away. They pulled into the white rock of her driveway before either of them said anything.

Nash swung the gearshift into park but didn't turn to look at her yet. "What. Was that?"

"Laramie 2.0." Roxy leaned her head back against the headrest, staring out the windshield at her house. She'd designed it herself, poured over every detail. An ache settled inside her at even the thought of leaving it. At the very *thought* of what Tag asking her to run away again, believing that all he had to do was sing and she'd fall into his open arms.

He turned his head to study her. "So. There's definitely more to your relationship with Tag than you let on—or what I guessed from what I knew, and you let me assume." The space between his eyebrows pinched.

She rubbed at her forehead. "He showed up, claiming to have loved me all along, but you know how he was in high school. Always another girlfriend." She tilted her head to the side to look at Nash, worried about how big of a deal this would be for him—like how he would feel listening to the videos of Tag's song being shared and blowing up social media. Tag had done something big, and it wouldn't blow over soon. Her running away likely would only add fuel to the fire.

"And what else, Rox?" Nash didn't reach for her hand or move to put his arms around her the way he'd shielded her back at the concert, and that said a lot about how tonight must have made him feel. "He just sang a song clearly begging you to come back to him."

"*Back* to him?" She gave a mirthless laugh. "I'd have to be with him in the first place to go back."

"Rox."

She sighed and closed her eyes. "I told you about how he came to see me in Laramie, right after he got his first contract and blew up. This was just that. Again. Same old Tag. It's not real." He'd told her that night that he'd been hiding, in a way, all through high school and that he was going to show her he meant it when he'd told her he loved her all those times. "He sang that song—not that stuff he added on at the last—but the rest of it. It's the only other time I've heard it."

Nash opened his door and got out, walking around the Jeep to open her door and pull her out into his arms. He stared down at her, brown eyes full of worry. It sliced through her heart that Tag's big, dumb gesture had done that to him. "Why didn't you go with him?"

Roxy crinkled her nose. "Why *would* I? All of the sudden he was saying he loved me. It came out of the blue." Nash snorted with laughter and Roxy scowled, leaning back her head to glare at her boyfriend. "What?"

"Everyone could tell he was in love with you back in high school, Roxy. Don't deny that."

She pulled out of his arms and headed across the grass toward her porch, waving away his words. "But he never told me. All that stuff he said in his songs? He's a musician. That's what they do. How was I supposed to know he meant any of it when he'd never said it for real? Especially when he took off and didn't talk to me for the eight years in between."

Silence settled between them for a long time, Roxy wondering what thoughts ran through Nash's head. "And now?" Nash finally looked up at her, but his expression was tight with whatever answers he'd come up with in the intervening moments.

She shook her head and threw a hand back toward the fair-grounds. "I never wanted that. Not when I was eighteen. Not now. I want home. I want Little River." She stepped back toward him. "I want you." Tag had only been able to imagine bright lights and making it big, none of which he needed Roxy for. He could say the words, but Roxy didn't know what he really meant by them.

She didn't reach out for Nash, to force him into coming to her way of seeing what had happened tonight. She waited him out, since she didn't know herself how she really felt about Tag singing that song, and the things he'd said, and what it meant that hurt had flooded through her from the first note until long after she ran away. How the words kept playing over in her mind and how she couldn't stop thinking of the first time he'd sung it to her.

When Nash still didn't say anything, she added quietly. "He believes that all it takes is a song and him asking for me to give up everything and walk away. But he doesn't understand real love." She folded her arms around her, determination growing. It joined the anger that had sparked earlier and the sting of how Tag had made Nash feel. What didn't Tag Turner understand about using a telephone?

She glared out at the mountains where she knew Tag would head once the show was over. "And it's about time I gave him the talking-to he's deserved for eight years."

CHAPTER THREE

Tag pulled the rental car into an empty space at the darkened look-out and settled back in his seat for a moment to enjoy the view of the valley below. Small batches of lights twinkled, outlining the small community of Little River and the nearby towns. This high on the mountain, he could see for fifty miles or more. He pushed open his door, grabbing the University of Wyoming ballcap on the passenger seat out of habit. It was nearing midnight. No one was likely to even be driving on the highway, let alone the small lane he'd taken to the look out and the trail head, so he didn't need to hide, but he shoved the cap on anyway. The fact that he always wore a ball cap was something he shared with both his personas.

He started down the thin strip of dirt that led to the trailhead. The trail up to the waterfall was an easy one, and with his flashlight, it wouldn't be a dangerous nighttime hike. There were certainly others on this mountain that he'd taken before that would be. But he only had this one night in Little River before his tour bus moved on to other towns in Wyoming, ending in Casper. Then he'd take at least six months to rest while he worked on his new album. The Hometown Tour had been a brilliant idea, and he'd enjoyed being back in Wyoming and the neighboring states. Not to mention the fact that they'd been hugely successful and the talk about it had ended up selling out the four big-city venues on the tour.

He should have suspected that it didn't matter what he sang, it wouldn't change Roxy's mind—but he'd hoped. Even though she'd ignored years worth of concert tickets that he'd sent to her in hopes that she'd just come and listen. For once *hear* what he was telling her.

But she hadn't, so now he needed to take this hike anyway and clear his head of her once and for all. He would be okay—over the years he'd learned to let go of the hurt that came with another heart-felt song he'd written for her that she ignored. With every year that had passed, missing her had become a little easier. The hope eroded little by little that she would hear something in one of his songs to make her finally understand. And little by little he'd been okay, even though he missed her like crazy.

When Beau scheduled the kick-off in Little River, Tag had decided to take one last shot. Even when he walked out on stage and found her hand in hand with Nash Roberts. Small towns. If she'd stayed here, he probably knew every single boyfriend she'd ever had by name.

"Tag Turner, how *dare* you."

He froze at the entrance to the trail, a smile spreading over his face. The way she'd stood stiffly next to Nash and then fled the concert without so much as talking to him had sparked a hope that at least she cared—and the anger in her voice? He could work with that. For the first time in years that spark inside him lit into a small flame; maybe he could finally make her love him enough.

He turned around, not bothering to wipe off the smirk. She was as gorgeous as ever. Long brown hair pulled up on top of her head, wispy strands waving around her face as she stalked toward him, arms swinging.

"How dare I what, Rox? Come back?"

"Sing *that* song in front of everyone. Say all that nonsense in front of the whole county and then some." She folded her arms, and leaned toward him, the way she'd lectured him a dozen times or more in high school.

"Including Nash?" he said dryly.

"*Especially* Nash," she snapped.

Tag took a step toward her, knowing that his tough girl wouldn't give an inch, and if he'd flustered her enough to make her run away, this ought to crank things up a few levels. "If Nash is such a big deal, what's the problem with me singing that song?"

She took a long breath in and then slowly let it out, shaking her head at him. "You've never sang it before and you suddenly decide to introduce it to the world the night you're back in Little River? And top it off with a crazy publicity stunt?"

"How would you know I've never sang it?" He tilted his head to the side, letting it go for now that she'd dismissed his pleas to love him. She'd never been to a concert that he knew of until tonight, and he'd like to hear her admit it right now. One long strand of her straight hair hung down almost to her shoulder and a breeze shifted it in front of her face. He wanted to reach up and push it aside, but Tag had known Roxy long enough to know that he had to let her anger simmer down before he stoked a different kind of flame.

"The internet is blowing up, every girl asking when the single will be released and who is Roxy Adams and why did she run away? And yet the Taggart Dubois camp has been strangely silent." Still, her jaw worked.

The fact that her anger hadn't diminished in the last few minutes made Tag even more hopeful. Why would it matter so much if it *didn't* matter? Sure, he'd made plenty sure she knew exactly what he was asking and exactly how he felt—and that meant everyone in the world would know pretty soon as well. But if she didn't love him even a little, why was she so worked up about it? Why wasn't she ignoring him the way she had the past eight years?

He kept a casual expression and reached into his pocket for his phone. Sure enough, Beau had called several times and texted, asking Tag what was with the new song. Tag put the phone back in his pocket.

"Well, guess the decision's made about whether to put that on my new album if it's so popular." He shrugged.

She cried in frustration and spun away from him. "You are the worst, Tag!"

"What's the big deal?" he repeated, shifting so he sat on the fence lining either side of the trailhead. "If you ever actually cared about that song, I expect you might have said something the last few years."

Just like that, she was back in his face, finger wagging. "You don't get to do that. You don't get to waltz in and out of my life with sweet words, *like you always do*, and act like it's my fault I didn't follow you like the puppy you wanted. You don't get to blow through my life and scatter everything before you blow right back out, *like you always do*."

He stood back up, using the six-inch height difference to his advantage, making her crane her neck and take a hurried step back when her flying hands brushed over his t-shirt. "You don't get to come in here like I haven't been begging for your love since day one, *like you always do*," he finished, in a tone matching hers.

"Ha." She folded her arms again and ducked her chin. "You expect me to fall at your feet because you sang some sweet lyrics but never showed me any truth to them?"

"I expected you to love me enough to understand when I said I love you." He flipped on his flashlight, spinning it toward the trail. Suddenly her temper wasn't attractive or the beginning of a spark. It only reminded him of the first time she'd heard that song, when she'd said he wasn't enough.

But he shed the disappointed ache. He'd had plenty of practice over the years pretending like Roxy casting him aside hadn't bothered him. Besides, it made for lots of mournful song material.

"Heading down to the waterfall," he said with a half-smile that had made many a woman go weak in the knees (just not ever Roxy). "You're welcome to come along." Then he turned his back on her and walked away.

<hr>

ROXY TOSSED and turned in the early morning hours, trying to banish memories of Tag from her mind and figure out why that man got under her skin so well.

. . .

"I'LL NEVER BE ENOUGH for you, no matter how famous I am," Tag had said when he stood at the door of her dorm room, hand on the door handle and ready to leave. His goodbye hung heavy in the air, a weight pressing against Roxy's chest, making it difficult to breathe. That thread that always stretched between them pulled tight, begging her to ease the tension along the line, to go to him, stay by him, lest the thread snap.

But she swallowed that temptation. Even if he meant what he was saying, once she followed Tag, that's all she'd ever do. She'd see the ranch—home—in fleeting glances over her shoulders, raise kids on a tour bus or in Nashville. She didn't want that life.

"You can't expect me to give up so much on so little," she'd said back, hanging onto her desk chair with one hand to keep her steady.

His eyes had narrowed and he'd shaken his head. A second later he'd stepped through the door. Girls in the common room outside gasped and she heard someone whisper his name.

Then the thread snapped.

She pulled a pillow over her head. Whether or not she had feelings for Tag was a moot point. Nothing he'd said last night led her to believe he was looking for an early retirement and a nice quiet life in their beautiful little hometown. Nothing he'd said made her believe anymore than she had back then that he honestly loved her.

She woke late the next morning and checked in with Bellamy before hopping in her truck and heading to town. When she got to the clinic, she parked in the back with the rest of the employees and slipped in the back door.

"How busy is Nash today?" she asked one of the nurses manning the desk.

"Swamped," the brunette said with a pitying glance at Roxy. Roxy bristled. She'd already read enough nonsense online from the locals and she wasn't particularly excited about experiencing it first-hand. "But he's in his office right now, so I bet you could sneak a minute," the nurse went on.

"Thanks." Roxy forgave the nurse her pity and hurried down the hall to Nash's office, tapping a couple of times before pushing the door open.

"I'm coming, I'm coming, Shelly. Just let me finish this one thing." Nash chewed on the end of a pen, one hand in his hair as he studied the paper in front of him. Roxy smiled as she admired him in the black scrubs he wore. His lab coat hung over the back of the chair, but more often than not, he forgot to wear it anywhere. He must have gone back and forth between the hospital a few times today to already be out of his slacks and dress shirt.

"Can you spare one minute for this little thing?" Roxy asked, shutting the door behind her.

Nash's gaze snapped up, and his customary smile flashed onto his face before it disappeared almost as fast. She rushed over before he got too far in his rememberings of the night before and sat on the edge of the desk.

"I'm really sorry about last night. I acted like an eighteen-year-old, maybe because somehow seeing Tag again brought me back there, and I didn't think. He upset me because that song used to mean something to me, but that's all in the past. Tag is gone, of course, and he's not coming back to Little River," she said hurriedly. Nash really only had a minute. She had to get this apology out as quickly as she could.

He studied her intently as she spoke, then said his next words cautiously. "Did you love him back then, when he came and asked you to come along?"

She hesitated over her words, cringing when Nash stiffened. "Maybe," she admitted. "It's hard to know what was hurt over him throwing away our friendship and what might have meant more. But that was a long time ago. He had to do something big when he came home. It's what people expect of Tag. It doesn't mean anything, not really to him. Especially not to me." She tilted her head in a plea for Nash to understand. They'd been dating for eight months, plenty of time to know each other. But in this quiet little town, they hadn't faced a disruption like Tag Turner before this. She wanted them to pass this test. "I'm sorry for the way things went down last night. You're here, and that's right where I'm desperate to be."

Nash stood, wrapping his arms around her waist. "Thank you, Rox. I understand it threw you for a loop. I wish you would have told me how much you didn't want to go to that concert." Even though it was a gentle scold, Nash had a way of making an apologetic tone wind through the words. This man was an angel. He bent over her, pulling her closer to him as they kissed. She wound her arms around his back, relaxing now that their fight had settled quicker than she'd hoped.

"Yeah," she murmured against his lips. "I should have said something. I didn't want to make it a big deal, but I see now I should've just been honest."

"Apology accepted." He smiled, continuing their kiss before he pulled away reluctantly. "I really have to go."

"I'm still feeling a little 'sick' over how I acted," she whispered, making Nash chuckle.

"I'd better investigate that very seriously."

She laughed with him, enjoying their moment, however brief. "Come over for dinner tonight?" she asked as she finally leaned back away from him.

"Of course. It's been a wild day, so I don't know how late." He brushed his fingers along her jawline, dropping a kiss on her cheek before he stepped back toward the door. "I'm sorry, hon, it's crazy."

She stepped toward him, drawing him back to her for one more kiss. "Thank you for the minute. And you've earned the right to be as late as you need to be."

"See you later." He opened the door and slipped out of the office. She followed him, her body relaxing by the second the more that his presence, even for a moment, filled her. There was a steadiness to Nash that she'd recognized from those first dates, and it reeled her in every day. She could picture, so easily, a happy, settled life with him. Being a doctor brought with it its share of crazy, but he didn't make her guess about his feelings and he didn't need grand gestures to show them.

Maybe Tag Turner really did love her and maybe he had written all those songs about her. The truth was, he'd never said it and that meant something.

CHAPTER FOUR

Tag lay on his bed as his tour bus rumbled down I-25, away from Casper and toward Denver. They'd finished up the last few stops on his Hometown Tour, which had been as successful as anticipated. Beau had arranged photo opps with people from Tag's past in every city, adding to the hype and excitement. Each Instagram post had been more liked, more commented on than the last, and the YouTube video he'd recorded of a soft, acoustic version of Roxy's Song—minus the begging at the end—had millions of views. In a fit of spite over how she'd reacted, he'd even titled it that. That's how he'd always thought of it in his head. Besides, after his stunt at the concert, everyone knew exactly who that song was about anyway. His conscious had been eased momentarily when a comment from Roxy popped up on the link to the video that his official Facebook page had posted.

I've always loved this song. Congratulations, Tag! Your friends are so proud of you. The fact that she hadn't answered the phone call he'd made after he saw it said that she'd posted it to keep the small-town gossip mill in Little River from blowing up over what the song meant, making everyone think his bid for her heart had been something for publicity. She hadn't responded to the crazy number of replies on her comment either, some asking if she was *the* Roxy. People in Little River kept answering with affirmatives. Everyone knew about Roxy being Tag's high school sweetheart.

You would've had to have dated me at least once to be that, wouldn't you? she would have said to him. Back in those days she'd laughed off every attempt he made to show her how he felt, saying she couldn't trust him to be serious. He'd never given her a reason to. And when he'd reminded her of all that the night he'd tried to make her follow him, she'd laughed then, too. *That was just flirting. You never followed it up with anything, and now you expect me to just run away with you on your word that you meant it all, all that time?*

The way the night sped by in dim shapes along this familiar freeway reminded him of road trips with Roxy. He'd make her drive and he'd sit in the passenger seat with his guitar, serenading her.

"Someday, I'll have to drive this road myself, only listening to you on the radio," she said.

He took her hand, kissing her fingertips until she pulled away and slapped at him. "Someday you'll be with me in my big ol' tour bus, darlin'." *She laughed at his fake southern twang and shook her head.*

"You'll never be serious about me. Especially not when every girl in America is throwing themselves at you."

"I'll always be serious about you," he hummed to himself and cast a longing look across his bed. Roxy wasn't here. He'd always assumed that eventually he'd have her company on these long trips or her sweet voice on a phone call to make it go by quicker. More words spilled into his head and he pulled his notebook closer. In the month since he'd seen her in Little River, he'd filled half the pages with lyrics, lines that Beau nodded over with pride when Tag let him hear a few. Roxy had always inspired his words in a way he couldn't make her understand. It was the hitch in their relationship. He spoke fluent country-love-song, and she only knew enough to get by. Didn't trust that his heart was in those words.

This could be his best album yet if he could hang on to how she made him feel. Even the way she'd lectured him burned inside him. He scribbled something about flames and lighting a match, then tapped his pen against his cheek as he tried to come up with words that rhymed. Patch. Snatch. He scowled out at the scenery. Ranch.

Ranch. He could make those words sound right in a song. He sang to himself, fitting it in, and grinned as he wrote it in the margin. Then it struck him harder.

He didn't have to rely on those fleeting moments with Roxy at the trailhead for Ten Falls. He strummed a few more chords, experimenting with the lines he'd written down, not surprised when they flowed through him like the creek that fed that waterfall. Laying down his guitar, he picked up his phone to text Beau.

I need a favor.

CHAPTER FIVE

"What's going on?" Roxy asked, poking her head into Bellamy's office and waving her phone around. "Something wrong?"

"Something's really right." Bellamy beamed, clasping her hands together on the desk. "How would you like to fill up the rooms at the ranch all the way through the end of September?"

Roxy put a hand on her hip and scowled at her manager. "This is something you always handle by yourself. Did it really warrant three different texts all asking me to get over here now?"

"This you're gonna have to approve. I just got a call from some hot shot talent manager asking if we'd rent the ranch out for at least three weeks to give some big star their privacy." Bellamy looked down at the notebook she kept on her desk to keep track of random notes. "In exchange for making sure they're not disturbed and that we don't disclose to anyone that they're out here, they're willing to pay a lot of money." As Roxy came forward and dropped into a chair, Bellamy handed her a sticky note. "Say, 'yes, thank you,' to funding your next pet project."

Roxy stared down at the figure on the sticky note, her lips spreading into a grin. The Arrow C had never hurt for money. She made a nice profit on the actual ranching business side of things; turning the old ranch house into a bed and breakfast and opening the ranch up to tourists had just been an expansion of an already thriving business, something that she'd done more for the community of Little River. Without a large source of jobs, the small town always teetered toward ghost town status. With money like this, Roxy could do even more for her beloved community. She could start thinking much bigger than she had been, maybe sink a little bit more money into one of these projects than she'd felt safe doing this far. And having someone famous slip word to their friends that the Arrow C valued their privacy? That wouldn't hurt business.

"Have you got any other bookings this would conflict with?"

"One." Bellamy glanced down at her notebook again. "But we could upgrade them to the cabin over at the Double A. Honeymooners from Utah, so I doubt they'll complain about the extra privacy. They hadn't booked any extra activities."

"You certainly have my approval. What's to say no to?" Roxy laughed. "Any ideas who it is?"

Bellamy shook her head. "The agent wouldn't say. Promised me a deposit as soon as I called back with a confirmation and all his information is legit. He insisted that he couldn't say his client's name and that we were to instruct our staff to stay out of the way as much as possible to avoid too many people finding out." She bit her bottom lip. "Do you think it's worth the trouble?"

Roxy nodded. "Yes. You'll be down to half staff by the end of August anyway." The Ranch House was still growing, with summer being the best time for business. By the time fall was ready to roll around, their bookings significantly dropped. Maybe that would change after their famous visitor. "How many people are they bringing in?"

"He said around ten." Bellamy scribbled a few more things on her notebook.

"You'd know better than me, Bell, but it definitely sounds like something we can handle with half staff." Roxy stood to leave Bellamy to make the arrangements.

Bellamy's face broke into a grin. "Who could it be, do you think?"

"Hopefully one of the Hemsworths." Roxy winked and headed back out of the office.

"If only!" Bellamy called after her.

As Roxy walked back through the ranch house, she eyed it with pride. Antique pieces from the home's long history littered every room, complemented by subtle western themes to pay tribute to the ranch and country chic décor that made the front room welcoming and professional at the same time.

She found herself wondering how their mystery celebrity had heard about her place and Tag flitted across her brain. He likely had a hand in mentioning it to someone, which turned Roxy's guesses from A-list actors to country stars. She quickly pushed the thoughts away though. In the weeks since seeing Tag, she'd successfully dismissed her concerns over her reaction to seeing him again. She didn't want to spiral back down into the questions, and she hated that she couldn't completely dismiss him from her mind. He lived in the corners of her heart, a tenant she'd never been able to fully evict even though she did a good job of ignoring his presence most of the time.

After he'd begged her to come with him, she had second guessed her decision too much, inklings of regret always threading through her. There was always the possibility he had meant every word just a deeply as he claimed. She just didn't have any evidence. And on top of that, she didn't want the life he led—always in the spotlight and on the road half the year. How much would she have even seen him if she'd chosen that path with him? Sure, at first, she could have traveled all over with him, but she would have turned bitter at losing her settled, predictable life. And if they'd decided to have a family? You couldn't take kids on the road.

Though her heart had hurt over turning him down, she'd made the right decision all those years ago—and again, six weeks ago. Tag had always lived in a world where his romantic notions made sense. Roxy didn't live in that world.

For the first time since Bellamy told her, unease prickled in Roxy's stomach. Even if their mystery guest knew Tag and had been recommended to the ranch by him, that didn't mean that Roxy had to struggle with her decision all over again.

She'd make sure of that.

CHAPTER SIX

When the suburban pulled up in front of the Arrow C Ranch House, Tag kept his seat for a moment and stared at it. It was just like Roxy to choose a simple, yet classic name when she'd turned it into a bed and breakfast. Roxy had grown up in this huge house and so Tag had spent a good deal of time there as well. The perusing he'd done online showed that she'd kept much of the house the same, structure-wise. Still sixteen rooms, like they'd always touted the Victorian-era mansion at the local museum. Roxy's fourth great-grandfather had built it for his wife when they'd moved out west from New York in the 1800s and it had stayed in the family for seven generations now. It was on the county register of historic homes, although the inside didn't look anything like the pictures Tag had seen from its early days. Each generation had updated the home and kept it up, so the décor had changed over the years. Roxy's mom had worked with the antique pieces that had remained with the house, but it had always been a stylish mix of modern and classic. Roxy had kept that look, so the pictures on the website had taken Tag back to the days when they would lounge on the big sectional in the open living area that looked into the kitchen. That homey look was still there, although the dining table looked newer and much less lived on. The

Ranch House boasted that visitors could spend the weekend as special guests of the family.

"So this is the place where you're going to write your greatest album yet," Beau said from beside him, snapping Tag out of his reverie.

"This place holds a lot of memories," Tag assured him, same as he had been for the last several weeks. Beau hadn't argued with Tag's proposal that they all take a nice vacation, nor the venue once Tag explained what it would do for his creative juices. He did mind the out-of-the-way location and the fact that Little River did not have a Starbucks.

"It's beautiful." Tag's assistant, Quinn, leaned over the seat to get a better look out the windows. "Do I get to ride a horse?"

"If you want to," Beau said. "Tag's got the whole thing rented out just for us, and since he's supposed to be taking it easy, maybe you can too."

Quinn grinned.

"You scared she's gonna kick you out?" Beau turned to Tag and asked in a low voice, smirking himself.

"She's not going to kick me out," Tag said. That was a bluff. She could *try* but Tag doubted the Ranch House manager would let her. They wouldn't be able to replace the guests that they must have turned down to accommodate Tag renting out all the rooms to have privacy.

He pushed open his door the same time Roxy and another woman stepped out onto the porch. The woman with chin-length brown hair waved, but her hand froze in mid-air when Tag got out of the suburban. It wasn't until Roxy yanked the woman's hand down that she came to life again.

"Welcome to the Arrow C," the woman called, hurrying down the steps ahead of Roxy, who glared daggers in his direction. The woman glanced over her shoulder, then rushed up to Beau. "You must be Beau? I'm Bellamy, the manager."

"Yep, that's me," Beau said, shaking her hand.

"Mr. Dubois." Bellamy's smile wavered when she turned to Tag.

Bellamy Hansen. It had taken him a second to place her. "I know I'm a few years older than you, but I don't think that means you need to call me Mr. I think, in fact, that you once called me Tag Turners-All-The-Girls-Heads, and I like that."

Beau choked on a laugh as her face turned red. But she laughed too. "Oh, middle school. Such a special time," she said. "This way." She gestured for them to follow as she headed back toward the house.

"Are we going to be allowed to stay?" Tag asked under his breath.

Bellamy forced another laugh and didn't answer.

"What a surprise," Roxy said dryly when they got to the porch. She held out a hand for Beau, which he shook. "Welcome to the Arrow C."

"Pleased to be here," Beau said, some of the amusement at the situation disappearing from his smile, turning it more professional. "Thank you for having us." Roxy raised an eyebrow, but got the door for them, and Quinn, who had followed them up on the porch. Tag's intern, Winnie James, still stood by the suburban, waving her phone around to try and get service. Someone ought to tell her that her big-city, cheap phone plan wouldn't work out here in Wyoming. Tag's bodyguard, Morgan, glanced back at her before following his employer into the house. So far, no crazy fans, so hopefully he'd get a vacation too.

Bellamy walked in ahead, pointing them to the stairs that still dominated the open space of the living area at the front of the house. "We've got you all spread out over the upper two levels, but make sure to let us know if any special arrangements need to be made. I think I covered everything Beau let me know about—" She glanced over at Morgan. He'd want the room next to Tag's. "But we're happy to change things up to accommodate anything else. Sweetie?" Bellamy looked past Tag to Winnie, who still held her phone up. "There's only two providers that work out here, Verizon and a local company. If you don't have either of those, give up." Winnie scowled and pocketed her phone.

"It's called a vacation, Winnie," Tag heard Quinn murmur.

Bellamy studied the group and turned back to Beau. "I thought there would be more of you."

"The band will show up maybe for a week or so and we'll have some crew in to do casual videos and live feeds we have planned to hype the album, but for most of the time, just us," Beau answered as they trooped up the stairs after Bellamy. Tag glanced over his shoulder to see if Roxy followed. She was chatting with Quinn as they came up, so studious about not looking his way that he knew she was avoiding having to talk to him.

Bellamy doled out rooms as they walked along the hallway before she came to one of the biggest on this floor—Tag knew since he and Roxy had hosted plenty of games of hide and seek out here in their early high school years. The big house had been a blast, with so many nooks and crannies to hide in. The number of times he'd cornered Roxy in some small space, intending to confess his feelings were too many. So was the number of times he'd chickened out. A little voice in the back of his mind had whispered for years that's why she didn't believe him when he did finally get the nerve. He clenched his jaw. He'd sang enough songs with her as the star, back in high school and since then, to heap the evidence in her lap.

Bellamy pushed open the door to the familiar room. "Mis—Tag, we've got you here—"

"But you can switch out for another one on the floor if this is weird," Roxy broke in. She forced a smile, like she was trying to come off calm, but she glanced away after she'd said it and winced.

"Why would this room be weird for him?" Quinn, who had been given the room across the hall from Tag's bodyguard, stuck her head out of her door.

Tag's face broke into a smile as he met Roxy's gaze and held it. "This used to be Roxy's room growing up. And I think I'll be very comfortable in here."

He waited for the outburst to come, for Roxy to declare him *the worst* again. And steam was for sure about to spit out her ears, but Bellamy laid a hand on her arm and Roxy took a deep breath. "I grew up in this house," she said to Quinn. Disappointed in her bland response, Tag strolled into the room, the discussion with his assistant about how Roxy had opened the bed and breakfast and then built her new house fading behind him.

He didn't understand why Roxy was so bent out of shape about him taking this room. It looked nothing like what it had when Roxy had lived here. It still had the same shape—a big, open square with tall windows facing the mountains—and the best view, which is why Bellamy had picked it for their mystery celebrity, no doubt. The personal bathroom and walk-in closet sat on the opposite side of the room as the windows.

But the décor was completely different. Denim blue headboard with big gray buttons had replaced Roxy's rustic wooden one. And instead of bedding and linens in shades of pink, everything was gray and blue. In the corner, where her desk had been, there was a gray café table and two upholstered, blue arm-chair stools. The dresser was much bigger than Roxy's old one and refinished in a distressed ivory. The light fixture hanging in the middle of the room was new as well, an iron and glass thing that twinkled in the sunlight from the windows. In the final corner of the room, there was a fluffy gray couch, chair, and ottoman.

He could already picture himself spread out on the couch and ottoman, guitar in hand, strumming, Roxy leaning up against his chest...

He let the daydream linger.

"Do you like it?" Roxy asked.

It took Tag a second to realize that Roxy stood in the room with him, really asking him the question. It held an edge, but her eyes said she wanted to know.

"It's really nice, Rox," he replied. "Everything here is beautiful. That's why I knew it would be the perfect place to write my album— that and you're here." When he'd first answered he wanted to play nice, to ease Roxy into admitting she loved him as much as he did her, but like always, he couldn't help the comments that spilled out of him around her. For years he'd been able to say whatever he wanted. She'd never taken his devotion seriously, whether it came in flirtatious comments backed by the truth or in songs, so it never mattered.

"This was a horrible trick to play," she snapped in a low voice.

He sighed. He was tired of her anger, even if it meant he affected her more than she wanted. "This is home," he said, and held up his hands when she huffed at him. "Little River is home. Whether you believe it or not, you are the inspiration behind my best music and being here in July showed me this place can really light a fire under my muse. The Ranch House is the only place that could have accommodated me with the peace and quiet I needed to get the writing done without interruption."

She chewed on her lip, indecision in her expression. About whether to believe him about her being an inspiration? "You could have been honest."

He stuck his hands in his pockets and eyed her. "You wouldn't have let me come."

They stared at each other for several seconds and she didn't argue with that assumption. "Just so you know," she said, her voice going cold again. No, not cold. It was more like forced indifference. "I don't work here at the Ranch House. You won't be seeing me all that much."

Tag pointed out the window, toward the white house off in the distance, its gables and wraparound porch and the white brick simultaneously matching both the rustic landscape around it and the proud Victorian mansion they stood in. "I'll see you just as much as I need to." He smirked.

Roxy whirled and stalked out of the room, the long sigh she released saying exactly what she hadn't. *Tag Turner, you are the worst.*

CHAPTER SEVEN

Roxy resented the fact that Bellamy was pushing her out of her own house.

Okay, so not exactly her house anymore. And no, she didn't live there, but she did own it.

"Go on and get yourself some lunch. Maybe in town?" Bellamy said. "I've got things covered here."

Roxy resisted one more time, folding her arms as Bellamy tried to nudge her out the door. "I behaved!" she protested.

Bellamy nodded, not letting up. "Considering Tag Turner showed up on your doorstep, yes you did. But considering how you treated guests of the Arrow C? No, you did not. Go to town. Cool off. I don't need you back here so there's no reason to be here and let him twist you all up."

Roxy stepped out onto the porch. "I am *not* all twisted."

Bellamy arched an eyebrow but didn't respond. "Tag will always talk up the Arrow C because you own it, but his manager, Beau? And the assistant and intern? They don't know your history—maybe Beau does. He sort of looked like he might"—she waved away that consideration—"but the others don't. And they don't know why the owner acted like someone had left manure on the front porch when someone as big as Taggart Dubois just crossed the threshold."

Roxy blew out a breath. Bellamy was right. Had anyone other than Tag showed up, she would have bent over backward. She still should have, for his entourage if nothing else. She'd posted that sweet comment on his Facebook page, hadn't she? She could do the same here. Show people, especially people in this town, that the song meant nothing. That Tag showing up here meant nothing.

"All right. I'm sorry."

Bellamy's shoulders relaxed. "Good girl."

"I don't think I'm going to make it through this month, not with the new season of *The Catch* not starting until October." She scowled. Watching a famous athlete work his way through dating eight women on the popular TV show was one of Roxy's biggest stress relievers, and after everything with Tag, she could use a reminder that someone's life was far more dramatic than the crazy world she'd dropped into since Tag's concert in July.

"Just think, you're gonna deserve the reward." Bellamy grinned and side-hugged Roxy as they headed for the door. "Watch Dan Jackson's season. You know you love it and it will make you feel better."

"Excellent idea."

Bellamy laughed and waved as Roxy headed around the building to her truck parked at the back. Her house was only a quarter mile down the road, but she hadn't wanted to walk up this morning when she'd come to help Bellamy prepare.

"So who is it?" a low voice asked, making Roxy nearly jump out of her shoes.

"Nash!" she cried, putting her hand to her heart. "You nearly gave me a heart attack." She grabbed his hand and yanked him around the back of the building before one of Tag's people saw him. They'd promised not to allow other people besides employees on the property during the weeks they were here. "You're not supposed to be here," she scolded him.

Nash's eyes only brightened. "So, it's someone who's a big deal? Like a really big deal?"

She let out a giggle. Oh, it felt good not to clench her fists and swallow back accusations after the last twenty minutes. She let Nash's excitement relax her. "You know I'm not supposed to talk about it."

"What if I guess? Was Bellamy right? One of the Hemsworths?" He rubbed his hands together, trying to peer around the corner she'd just pulled him around.

Roxy glanced up at the windows above her. Tag's room—her old room—was just above them. Sure enough, the curtains shifted when she looked up. She pressed her lips together. Would Tag tell his manager? He had every right to demand Nash leave the property. It was in the contract. Only employees of the Arrow C and Double A Ranches were allowed, and every single one had to sign a nondisclosure statement, including Roxy. Nash might be her boyfriend, but she wouldn't put it past Tag to have him banished from the property to clear the way for himself—at least in his mind.

"It's Tag," she said in a dry voice.

The excited glow to Nash's expression extinguished like someone had thrown a wet blanket over a campfire. "Are you kidding?"

The unease that had threaded through her the night of her concert came back, reminding her how hurt Nash had been over Tag's actions. "He says he wanted to write his new album in his hometown, and the Ranch House is the only place that could keep people away or something." She took hold of Nash's tie—he was wearing a dress shirt today —and pulled him down to her. "Lucky for me, I don't need to work every day at the Ranch House, and I don't have to see him." She smiled reassuringly at her boyfriend and then kissed him. That would show Tag if he was still spying.

I'll see you as much as I need to. She made the voice whiny in her head. *Get a load of this, Tag Turner.*

When Nash pulled away, he scrutinized her, and heat radiated out of her cheeks. Had he somehow read her mind and known the reason she'd chosen to kiss him right then? He didn't glance up at the window, so probably not, but shame pounded through her anyway. What was she doing?

"You worried you're going to fall for his charm?" Nash squinted down at her, the same hesitancy coming over his expression as the night she'd ran away from the concert.

"Of course not." It didn't matter what nonsense Tag came up with while he was here, Roxy's heart was with Nash in Little River, and it would stay there.

"Then why are you running away so hard?" Nash pulled back and scrubbed a hand through his hair. "Why not treat him like any other guest, Rox?"

"I would, but I'm sure he plans to use this as an opportunity to win me back. Doesn't that bother you?" She drew in a long breath, trying to sound indifferent about the whole thing. Why did Tag have to keep shaking things up for her? Why couldn't he just let her live the nice life she'd mapped out for herself? Instead, he had to stress her out with worries about how this would affect her relationship and how to make sure Nash knew how much she loved him.

Nash shook his head, frustration pulling at his frown. "It does, but only because you're acting like if you don't steer clear of him, you're in danger of falling for it." His expression was so sad it made Roxy lean forward toward him and grab his hands. "This is not you," he said, confusion lacing his tone. "Is this all such a big deal to you that you can't let it go? The concert stuff. Avoiding his songs and hurrying by that video anytime it comes up in your feed…"

I've always avoided his songs, she thought, but now wasn't a good time to bring that up. "Nothing is going on with me. I'm just surprised and unsettled. It will be fine."

Nash pulled his hands back and put them in his pockets. "You remember how I dated Addy in high school?"

Roxy scowled. "Of course."

But Nash didn't even smirk like he usually did if Roxy's jealousy reared because Addy's name came up for some reason. "Sometimes things are awkward when we go to the diner and she's working, but I don't get up and run out of the room. Or avoid the diner at all costs because she might try and get back together."

"She *does* bring extra whipped cream every time you order the pancakes." It was petty, but Roxy needed some leverage here.

Nash gave a dry snort of laughter. "You're overthinking this so much. I don't know what to make of it."

Tag's words came flooding back to her. *Why does it matter so much if Nash matters so much?* "What are you saying?"

He gave a shrug and a small smile that reeked of uncertainty. He leaned in and kissed her cheek. "It's worrying me that you're putting so much effort into running away from him." He turned and walked toward his Jeep, parked next to her truck.

"Hey, wanna have lunch?" she asked.

He grimaced. "I used my lunch hour to come out here. I'll see you tonight." He waved and got in, pulling around the Ranch House and onto the county road that led to the highway and into town.

She slumped against her truck and thought about what Nash had said. Stop running away from Tag. She could do that.

This was going to be a long three weeks.

CHAPTER EIGHT

Tag was definitely going to sell his Nashville house and move to the Ranch House full time. First of all, the cook was fantastic. Someone to rival the great Mrs. Garriott, who had her own spot at the town museum, her cooking had been so good. When he'd called down at 8:00 a.m. to ask Bellamy the breakfast options, she'd asked what he wanted. His only request was something hearty. Forty-five minutes later a plate had arrived stacked with light, flaky biscuits and creamy gravy, perfectly crisp bacon, and fluffy scrambled eggs. Tag had moaned softly to himself the entire time he ate.

A person wouldn't think so, but a wonderful meal like that had inspired Tag to finish the song he'd started on the flight out from Nashville. It may have included something about biscuits, but country music listeners appreciated a good biscuit better than anyone he knew, really.

Second, after his breakfast (and finishing the song), Tag had sat on the couch and stared out the big window at the mountains and grinned to himself. It surprised him how much he'd missed those mountains. The hikes he'd taken with Roxy and the numerous times he'd tried to declare his feelings in song at the top of some trail they'd taken (Roxy was always more fluent in country-music-romance after she communed with nature). Camping trips he'd gone on with his dad (He'd better call his mom and tell her to come out and see him). The whole idea of those mountains invigorated him. He scribbled down some thoughts before heading into the bathroom for a shower.

When he came down the staircase, it surprised him to see Roxy sitting with Quinn and Bellamy at the big dining room table, all three women in intense conversation over something on Quinn's iPad. He figured after the scene Roxy put on yesterday, he'd have to hunt the girl down to see her again.

"Good morning, ladies," he said, drawing their attention up to him. He stumbled when Roxy flashed him a smile along with the other two. Had aliens abducted his former best friend in the night and replaced it with some poor imitation? Roxy hadn't smiled so easy like that at him since before that fated night in Laramie.

"How was your breakfast, Mr.—Tag?" Bellamy grimaced at the title she'd given him and stood.

"I haven't eaten food so good in years. Maybe not ever." He rubbed at his stomach. "I'm really looking forward to lunch. Introduce me to the chef, because I plan to write an entire song in tribute to the skills."

Bellamy's face turned beet red and she raised her hand.

"Really?" Tag started in surprise. "You cook and manage?"

"Not usually." She gave a forced, embarrassed laugh. "Our usual cook is a snow bird who spends her winters down in Arizona. We let her off early this year so we could pare down the staff."

"She can't be better than you." Tag shook his head, incredulous that the backup had served him such an amazing breakfast.

"She taught me everything I know." Bellamy grinned at him. "She's my mom."

Tag couldn't help casting a look over at Roxy. "Looks like I need to frequent this place some more to be the judge of that."

Roxy kept her smile in place. "You won't be disappointed either way, Star."

A grin swept across Tag's face the same time his stomach swooped with a sense of triumph. She had given him that nickname the first time she'd heard him sing. What had changed to make Roxy accept his presence? To go so far as to allow some of their old friendship to slip back in?

"I'm thinking of hiking up to Paintbrush Springs. Wanna come?" he asked.

"Uh…" Roxy cast a panicked look over at Bellamy, the first hint that her easy demeanor with Tag might be an act. "Let me check what's on my schedule today and get back to you. Bell? Will you show me that thing you asked me about earlier? In your office?"

"Yeah, of course." Bellamy's answer came suspiciously quick, as suspiciously quick as Roxy's march across the lobby to the small office behind two French doors. Roxy forced a smile as she yanked shut the curtains to cut him off from view.

"What have you all been up to?" Tag asked Quinn when they'd been left alone.

"Just chatting with Roxy and Bellamy about some projects Roxy wants to take on for the ranch. I happen to know some people that Roxy's interested in learning more about." Quinn flipped closed the folio she kept her iPad in and trotted across the room toward the stairs.

"Like what?" Tag asked, intrigued. He followed, but conveniently stopped near the doors of the office, where he could hear Bellamy and Roxy's voices.

"Nothing to do with official Taggart Dubois business, so you can keep your nose out of it unless Roxy wants to tell you." Quinn smirked and hurried up the stairs.

Tag didn't follow and push the issue, especially since with her gone, he could slide closer to the office and listen in on Roxy and Bellamy.

"The thing is, I would take any other guest on this hike," Roxy said.

"Then go. Prove to Nash and you and Tag that you and Tag are just friends." Bellamy's voice had a hint of exasperation.

"I just don't know…" Roxy protested.

The swooping in Tag's stomach crash-landed and blew up some-where near his knees. So her attitude was an attempt to show her

boyfriend that things were fine between her and Tag—not a conse-
quence of her changed heart.

He clenched his jaw. No matter. He could work with that. If Roxy
let him have a foot in the door, he'd find a way to kick it open.

"Fine. Okay," Roxy said, her voice near the door, clueing Tag into
the fact that he'd missed Bellamy's response and that Roxy was soon
to find him eavesdropping. He took a few quick steps toward the
couches in the middle of the living room, and stood near one of the
wooden end tables, stained in a worn, gray tone. Like his room
upstairs, the main room of the Ranch House exuded that modern
country-chic look that made the house feel homey and welcoming. He
pulled out his phone to text Morgan about his plans, letting him know
that Tag wouldn't need him. The Ranch House had kept their promise
about things being a secret, and Tag doubted he'd need Morgan at all
on this trip. If he didn't want to stick around, maybe Tag should send
him home to spend time with his family. Tag wouldn't mind moving a
few notches up on Morgan's mom's favorites list, although considering he'd showed up unannounced to sing at her and Morgan's
father's fiftieth wedding anniversary party, he was pretty high as
it was.

"I'd love to join you on that hike," Roxy said, coming out of the
room.

Tag turned, putting his phone in his pocket and smiling back at
her, the same easy one she'd flashed him when he first came downstairs. "Perfect. I'll grab my things and we'll head up."

She nodded, and since he knew this was an act, he caught her
swallowing in nervousness as he headed toward the stairs. His mind
spun with a few words as he climbed the stairs, thoughts he could
work on as they hiked to help him convince Roxy that the right place
for her was with him.

CHAPTER NINE

Roxy squeezed the steering wheel as Tag carefully placed a ukulele case in the backseat of her pickup along with a small backpack. She'd texted Nash about twenty minutes ago, a simple *Headed on a hike up Paintbrush. Tag wanted to see it again.*

She hadn't heard back from him yet, but this ought to go a long way in proving she could be normal with Tag again. Paintbrush had been one of her and Tag's favorite trails back in high school. It was easy enough that it made for a relaxing afternoon when they had taken it, but long enough to give them some quality time together. Roxy had made sure to grab some headphones so she could avoid listening to Tag's humming and strumming as they hiked. He'd come up with some truly amazing songs back in their high school days when they'd taken hikes like this. Plenty that she'd caught snippets of on the radio before she shut it off, or the ones she'd heard on his first album, back before she turned him down and stopped listening to his music to dull the ache of missing him. She didn't know what wounds it would open up if she started hearing him again.

Tag stared out the window for the first ten minutes of the drive as they took the county road deeper into the ranch before they hit another county road and made the climb up into the mountains.

Roxy's phone ringing interrupted their silence, and she glanced at the caller ID listed on the screen of her truck—her sister, Taylor. She glanced over at Tag and moved to press the reject button, but Tag pushed her hand away, making her skin burn at the touch, and tapped the accept button.

"Miss Taylor Adams, to what do we owe the pleasure?"

"Who is that—are you with Nash? He sounded just like Tag for a second," Taylor said.

Roxy cringed and didn't dare look over at Tag after the reference to her boyfriend. Why was she even worried? Of course Taylor would assume it was Nash and not the man that Roxy hadn't spoken to for years. "It is Tag."

"Tag!" Taylor cried in excitement. "What are you doing with Roxy?"

"What kind of question is that?" He pretended to be offended. Roxy could picture the way her sister's eyebrows must be high on her forehead by now. She knew every bit of history between the two of them. Even though Taylor was nearly five years older than Roxy, they'd grown close after Taylor graduated and went to college. Their mother attributed that to no longer having to live in the same house together and to Roxy losing her ability to steal Taylor's clothes.

"Tag, be serious. How is it you get to be lucky enough to hang out in Little River?"

"Born lucky, sweetheart. The only thing that would be better is if you were here."

Roxy rolled her eyes at Tag's flirting, the ridiculous way he'd always gone over the top with both her and Taylor. Only back then, Taylor had bantered back and forth with him, unlike how Roxy would roll her eyes and dismiss him as a flirt. More often than not, Taylor's side of flirting with Tag included heavy reminders of their vast age difference.

"You're full of it, Tag Turner. Like always. I've got a baby now and I'm married to a man you could only dream of being as handsome as."

Roxy snorted. "I wish you could see how wounded he looks right now, T." It was so natural to slip into this mode with him. The words surprised her at how easy they were to say, the way that once she'd smiled at him that morning, her lips just kept on smiling with him like they always had. She'd just have to make sure real quick that her lips knew that smiling was the limit of what they could do where it concerned him.

"You two *do* know that I've been voted Country Music's Sexiest Star four times, right?"

"Psh." Taylor groaned. "If country music ever laid eyes on Gavin, they'd have to rename the honor Second Sexiest Star after Gavin Bennett."

"You tell 'em, honey." Gavin's voice came from the background, making all of them laugh.

"So…" Taylor said. "What's going on?" Roxy avoided looking over at Tag since curiosity was dripping off Taylor's voice the way Bellamy smothered her biscuits in butter.

"Roxy has a pretty little ranch out here that seemed like the perfect place to write a new album. We're hiking Paintbrush today," Tag answered.

"Awww. I love that trail. I can't tell you how jealous I am. It makes you rethink city life, doesn't it?"

Roxy tilted her head at the nostalgic tone Taylor had taken, the same nostalgia that had wafted off her post about Tag's concert back in July and how she couldn't be there. She'd never heard her sister miss Little River so much. Gavin had grown up in Denver, and before having Tucker, they'd travelled to cities all over the globe for Gavin's job. She thought Taylor thrived on her new city life. At least that had been the vibe Roxy got whenever Taylor subtly suggested that Roxy wouldn't shrivel and die if she ever wanted to think twice about rejecting Tag or moving to Nashville to be with him.

Tag glanced out the window at the trees passing by. "It sure does," he agreed.

"What do you need?" Roxy broke in. The last thing she needed was Taylor convincing Tag to spend even more time back in Wyoming.

"Oh, I was just calling about Christmas to see what your plans were. I think we're gonna come home."

"Oh?" Roxy sat back in surprise. "I thought you were all gung-ho on going to Rio and staying out of the cold."

"I miss Christmas on the ranch, but we'll talk about it later. I don't want to hog your catching up time with Tag."

Roxy gripped the steering wheel harder at the insinuations in *that* statement and avoided Tag's gaze. "Don't tell anyone he's here, T," Roxy said before her sister hung up. "It's a big secret. We all had to sign nondisclosure statements."

"Sexiest Country Music Stars tend to attract big followings," Tag interjected.

Taylor snorted. "My lips are sealed. You two have fun."

"Thanks!" Roxy said too brightly and hurriedly jabbed at the end button before Taylor got specific about the kind of fun the two should have. Tag glanced over at her with a smirk.

He turned back to the window, leaning forward as they passed a large meadow rising in the distance, a herd of elk nestled into the horseshoe shape of it. "You think you'll keep your land pristine for the rest of your life?" he asked in a soft voice. The almost-reverence in his tone sort of startled her. The ranch had been a bitter thorn in their relationship for much of their friendship. He'd always teased her for having "too-deep roots" in their small town and not being able to accept that she might like somewhere else just as much—somewhere like Nashville with him. He'd thrown that accusation at her that night in Laramie, and only then did she recognize how he might have meant it all those times before. That she was so stuck in Little River she didn't even consider what their future together could be.

And she hadn't. He'd always been bound for stardom, so perhaps that had never allowed her to recognize all those times he'd insisted he loved her that he might have been telling the truth.

"I don't know," she answered honestly. "I don't want to do anything like develop it with houses or something like that. I don't think the area could support that kind of thing—maybe some vacation homes, but that doesn't seem right." She gave a sigh, expecting him to scorn her old-fashioned sense of land ownership.

"No," he agreed.

She turned to study him. Was this part of Tag's tactic? Making overt attacks on her heart with his flirting and music while subtly sneaking his way in with supposed changes of heart over her family's legacy?

But he still stared out the window, a look of total concentration on his face, like he was seeing the land for the first time ever. Or seeing it the way Roxy had all her life. So that made the next words slip out of her mouth, and she was suddenly confiding in him the way she would have eight years ago.

"Four Star Energy wants me to lease mining rights for a vein of coal over by the old McKenzie cabin."

"It would make a lot of money." He turned toward her, but to her relief, his tone held the same hesitancy that wound through her every time she thought of the offer.

"It doesn't feel right either," she confessed. "I don't think it's enough to be worth it. Feels like they would come in, sweep it out, and leave a mess behind them to ruin my pretty ranch." She softened this observation with a smile and shrugged.

"Sounds like Quinn is trying to help you out with some other ideas?" He leaned his shoulder against the window and turned toward her.

The way he talked about this, like he cared that she cared, scared her—scared her because it seemed like he finally might understand the life she'd chosen. Not that he wanted it for himself, or maybe didn't even want it for her, but that he didn't blame her as much anymore. And if he didn't blame her, she couldn't really keep blaming him.

If all that anger died away... she might only be left with the feelings she'd been running away from since he ran away from her. Had all that hurt for him ignoring her all this time stemmed from the fact that she *did* love him more than as her best friend and not just because he'd exploded their friendship and run off when it didn't turn out his way?

"She asked me what I thought about a solar utility project. They have something down in Sweetwater County that sounds interesting."

She kept her eyes glued to the road, not ready to face any more of this "like we're still normal" conversation head on.

"That sounds more like you."

Roxy gripped the steering wheel again. Tag had a tone, soft and sort of husky. It came out in some of his more romantic songs and it had been a driving reason she stopped listening to him. A week after he'd walked out on her in Laramie, a song came on the radio with a slow section where his voice rasped over some painfully sad lyrics, lyrics she'd known she must have inspired with her many clueless rejections. It had stripped away all her high-road justifications for refusing to follow his dreams, showed her in that one moment the broken-hearted man she'd pushed away. Made her worry that she *had* loved him just like he'd said he loved her.

She'd turned off the music app on her phone and never listened to him again—always skipped to the next song the moment she heard the familiar openings of his songs in a playlist. And when the new ones started coming, from the first note she recognized his voice. She'd even spent a year or so immersed in pop music, but he would always show up there too with his many cross-over hits.

"Yeah," she said in a quiet voice and drew back in on herself. And even though she spent the rest of the thirty-minute drive up to the Paintbrush Springs trail reminding herself to keep things normal, she couldn't bring herself to start up a conversation again. To risk him sweet-talking her and finally making her believe it. And he didn't press her with more conversation. The one glance she snuck of him showed him staring out the window, one corner of his lips turned up in a smile.

When they reached the head of the trail, she pulled the small backpack she'd brought, filled with a water bottle, a couple of granola bars, and a jacket in case the summer day turned chilly. She was placing one of her earbuds in when Tag came up behind her and plucked the earbud out, making quick work of stealing her phone and holding it high above him.

"No electronics on the trail, Rox. You know the rules."

"Oh, no." Roxy shook her head and held out her hand. "Those rules don't apply."

He took a step forward, moving into her space and filling it up with his entire presence. Broad shoulders filled her view, making her tilt her head up to look at him. Tag had grown quickly in high school, reaching his full six-foot-four height by their senior year. But in eight years his shoulders and arms had turned much more muscled, the scruff over his chin that he'd let grow since he arrived clean-shaven yesterday, dark and sexier than the soft hairs he'd declared so much pride over back then. The eighteen-year-old boy that had wrapped her up in his arms, bent his head over hers to kiss her and beg her to come with him had made electricity hum through her. The man who stood before her now hadn't even touched her yet and every piece of her insides was on fire.

"Does that mean all the rules don't apply?"

Oh, that husky voice. *Don't run away. Don't run away. You have got this, Roxy Adams.* "Ha. Ha ha ha." The shrill, breathiness to her forced laugh gave away every one of her secrets. With every syllable, Tag's smile stretched wider and wider.

"ADMIT IT, Rox. Admit you love me." *They sat on the tail gate of her dad's pickup the night of graduation. He had on a smirk, so she rolled her eyes at his flirting. They'd just hiked the Ten Falls trail, one of their favorite night-time trails, and now Tag sat next to her, their shoulders and legs touching, keeping out the evening chill.*

"As big as these mountains," she'd said, waving a hand around her. They'd been best friends for well over four years now. Of course she loved him, though not like he always teased. "But it's not big enough." She hadn't meant for him to hear that serious thought. Thinking of him leaving her behind had hurt since he'd told her he was definitely leaving right after graduation.

He had leaned forward and pressed his forehead against hers. "That's plenty big. It's just that I love you more. As big as the stars." He pointed to the vast spread of twinkling lights above them, clearer on top of the mountains than anywhere in the valley below.

She thought of his plans. The duffle bag he had packed in his room. The close friendship she knew, just knew, would fade away with him leaving. "Then why are you leaving me?" she whispered.

"Why aren't you coming with?"

TAG TOSSED her phone and headphones onto the seat of her pickup, then turned and headed to the trailhead.

It was probably the worst decision she'd made in several years, but she left the phone behind.

CHAPTER TEN

T ag finally had Roxy walking along the edge with him again. Or
at least recognizing that they still had something there. He had
never in his life been a good strategist. His frequent confessions of
love for Roxy had come in impulsive moments, when his longing for
her had pushed him over an edge, and always in song because he
couldn't manage to get it out any other way. He'd never stopped to
think about how or when might be a better time, only that he had to
let her know. Even his decision to use the concert in Little River to
give it one last shot had been a spur of the moment thing with no
planning as to how best to present his case. Just told his band he was
going to play the next song by himself.

But that moment when he stepped up close to her, when he hadn't
been able to resist another second, when he'd almost given in and
scooped her into his arms—that was the moment he saw her flail
forward to the edge again instead of peering at him from her safe
perch. Something in that moment held him back and allowed him to
see that there might be something to having a plan.

He strummed aimlessly on his ukulele as they hiked the trail,
letting Roxy stay in her world and stew while he worked through a
plan in his mind. Every so often he'd sing soft lyrics just to watch her

shoulders relax for a moment and see her fingers flutter against her leg. Then she'd clench her fingers together and quicken her pace for a few minutes like she could outrun the way he made her feel.

She thought she was in love with Nash Roberts, and given her stubborn nature and the lengths she'd gone to avoid Tag up until this morning, he couldn't use a brute force attack on her heart and expect to come away the winner. He didn't like that getting Roxy back meant someone else losing her—he could understand how much that would hurt—but he couldn't live without her. So he had to sneak up on her, kind of like the way he had back at the car. Show her little by little how much he cared for her, how they were meant to be together, until before she knew it, she would take his hand and leap over the edge with him.

Like any time he spent in Roxy's presence, words pounded against him faster and faster. When he worried they'd burst out, against his new plan *not* to come at Roxy guns blazing, or that worse, he'd lose them, he found a rock at the side of the trail and stopped. He would sit and pull his notebook out of his bag to rest on his knee.

When he started strumming, for the first time, Roxy turned, maybe because the sound hadn't come from directly behind her. He sang a few words and scribbled them out, along with notes about which chords to use so he could remember.

"What about…"

Roxy's voice startled him as he realized she'd come to stand in front of him while he sang and wrote things down, but then she frowned when he brought his head up, and she took a step away. "Never mind." She shook her head, retreating further until she stood in the middle of the trail, hands on the straps of her backpack, waiting for him to finish.

She had been about to make a suggestion, like she had in the old days, the ones that Tag had always lapped up and hoped that meant she was starting to understand his language. He didn't push her. No more brute force attacks. He sang a little bit more, wishing she would've told him, wondering what she'd wanted to stay before she stopped herself. And finally, when he felt like he had enough down to at least capture the soul of the song, he closed the notebook and stood up.

"Sorry," he apologized as he packed his things away.

She shrugged. "You came back to Little River to write. I know this is where you got some of your best ideas."

"You're where I got some of my best ideas," he corrected, holding her gaze for a few seconds before trudging on. It killed him not to peek back to see how she'd taken his words. Having never planned an attempt like this before, he didn't have any idea if he was doing it right.

But those words felt right, and when the words felt right, he trusted that.

CHAPTER ELEVEN

M uch to Roxy's relief, Tag had gone inside as soon as they
pulled up to the ranch house. He'd hummed as he opened the
door for her truck, closing his eyes for a second and nodding to some
unheard beat before he hurried toward the house. He hadn't even
remembered to tell her goodbye or say anything else for that matter.
She recognized that obsessive drive to get the music down on paper.
She remembered the times she wouldn't hear from him for hours,
how he would ignore texts and calls, even when they'd already had
plans.

Then the relief fled as she drove back down toward her house and
couldn't get him off her mind, the way he'd stood so close to her and
the way his voice, his music, *him* could still wind inside her soul and
settle there. How all of that had happened and he hadn't done a thing
except for stand too close for a few seconds.

Yet here she was, running again. Going too fast down the lane
between the Ranch House and her home, like she couldn't flee the fear
fast enough. She hit the breaks and made a reckless u-turn on the dirt
road, dipping her truck down into the ditch on one side as she came
around. She parked in the back of the Ranch House and hopped out,
heading inside in search of Bellamy. She couldn't remember Nash

making her insides scorch the way Tag just had, but that was probably because they were settled now, comfortable with each other, an easy kind of electricity between them. Bellamy could help her remember that and help her turn on a fire hose to the heat raging through her even now just thinking about how close Tag had stood.

When Roxy peered around the mud room door to the dining area, Tag's crew sat around enjoying hamburgers and Bellamy's homemade fries. But Tag was noticeably absent. Thankfully. The last thing she needed right now was more muddied feelings and Tag resuming his sneaky campaign to convince her they were meant to be together. As she stopped and listened, behind the conversation she could hear faint guitar sounds from upstairs, explaining where he was.

"Looking for someone?" Bellamy asked, appearing in the doorway of the kitchen. Roxy's mother had always preferred to have the kitchen, dining, and living room open so their family could enjoy time together at meal times. But when they'd converted the house, Roxy had made some adjustments to the kitchen and dining area to wall the kitchen off from guests. The dining and living room still remained open, keeping that family-like atmosphere.

"You." Roxy crossed the hallway and pushed Bellamy back into the kitchen, which it looked like she'd been cleaning up after cooking. "First of all, just because we're supposed to keep a low staff, doesn't mean you need to do everything." Roxy shut the kitchen door behind her and spun on her friend. "Call Kassie in the morning and tell her to get out here to help with mealtimes. You don't have time for this."

Bellamy folded her arms across her chest and leaned against the large island in the middle of the kitchen. "Okay, Boss. What's the second of all?"

Roxy took a stool and sat down at the island, leaning forward to stare at her friend seriously. "When I first started dating Nash, the first time I kissed him, what did I say to you?"

Bellamy studied Roxy with confusion for several seconds, maybe waiting for Roxy to go on, then took a deep breath when she didn't. "That it was really nice. That you liked it."

Roxy swallowed. "I said that? I said nice? That I liked it? Did that make you suspicious in any way?"

Bellamy unfolded her arms and put her hands on her hips. "What's going on, Rox?"

Roxy could only moan in despair for a moment. It was worse than she thought. She had hoped that maybe that moment with Tag had somehow scrambled her memories or made her forget that when she and Nash first started going out, she'd felt that same electricity.

"Roxy."

She put her head in her hands and leaned over the island. "Today, right before we went on the hike, Tag got in my personal space—"

"Rox, just because he's famous and we signed all that stuff doesn't mean he can—"

Roxy held a hand up and raised her head. "And I thought I was on fire, Bellamy. I wanted him to hold me like he had in Laramie. I couldn't think about anything but kissing him for a good fifteen seconds, even though the other half of me was screaming to save myself. It was everything I'd forgotten existed when you *need* someone because I haven't had that with Nash, and I didn't even realize it."

Bellamy's mouth dropped open and she swore. "Girl…"

"I know."

"Nice…" Bellamy repeated and cringed. "Yes, maybe I should've been suspicious, but in my defense, I didn't know you as well in your Tag days. What are you going to do? You have to break up with Nash."

Roxy clenched her jaw. "I can't let Tag come in here and do this to me again. Fire might be nice and all, but people get burned and I can't throw myself at him over something like this, expecting it to actually be real."

Bellamy came forward and pulled Roxy's hands into hers, her expression getting soft. "I heard him singing right before I brought him his dinner. Something like, *I'm gonna wake up with you every day. I'm gonna count my blessings when I see your sweet face,*" Bellamy sang in a soft voice. "I stood there and let his fries get cold because it was so, so sweet. Like one of those songs you hear that makes you want to find your someone right now."

"He has always done that. I'm his muse, he says, but it doesn't mean anything." Roxy sighed and slumped back down to the table.

"It means something."

Roxy looked up at the meaning in Bellamy's voice, soft but a tone that dared Roxy to contradict her. "I'll talk to Nash. I'll be honest and we'll go on a break or something. But when Tag is gone, things will settle down and I can work things out with Nash. I'm sure of it." She stood back up and clenched her fists together. It seemed like Tag could make her love him again, just by showing up, but that didn't mean it would last.

⟡───────────────⟡

NASH'S JEEP was parked in front of the house when Roxy headed back. She slowed her truck. Bellamy was right. Not being able to get Tag off her mind wasn't fair to him. *I still have feelings for him,* she practiced in her head. She hated the sound of that on her tongue. Maybe those feelings were there, but she didn't want them to be. She didn't want to wonder what would happen when Tag went back to Nashville and his superstar life. Two declarations of love on either end of eight years didn't equal happily ever after.

When she came into her kitchen from the garage, Nash turned from where he set out plates on her dining room table. He laid down the forks and came toward her, his expression apologetic.

"What's up?" she asked, hoping she sounded calm and not like Tag had let loose a bunch of fire ants in her stomach. She would tell Nash they should take a break, but she didn't want to ruin the future by going into too much.

"I brought dinner." He wrapped her up in a tight hug and then pulled back to look at her. The fire ants scattered, thankfully. "I'm sorry about the way I said stuff this afternoon, that I made you feel like you had to spend the afternoon with Tag to prove he was just another guest or a friend and nothing more."

She swallowed. Nash had nothing to apologize for. "It's okay. I've missed hiking some of those trails."

Nash flinched, and it wasn't until she thought back on what she'd said that she realized she'd basically admitted to *not* hiking those trails in the years since Tag had left. She let the inference go. Trying to explain would only make things worse. Her love for Tag, even if she had thought it just friendship back then, hadn't been just as big as those mountains, it had been *in* those mountains and every place they'd walked together. Every song that came from those moments.

Nash leaned his forehead down onto hers. "I can't imagine having to spend the afternoon with Addy, and how awkward that would be. And I'm not even mad at her about things that happened between us." He closed the distance and kissed Roxy, and it was several moments later that Roxy realized that while the fire ants had left, nothing had replaced them. Just as she'd feared.

As she kissed Nash, nothing drove her to pull herself closer, closer, closer to him the way her feet had begged her to step forward and put herself in Tag's arms. Nash was a good kisser and she'd always enjoyed kissing him, but could she say that it was electric? Had it ever been?

"We need to talk," she murmured when he pulled away. The fire ants had returned, crawling up through her stomach and spreading over her chest, squeezing the life out of her.

His eyebrows squished together. "About the hike today? Tag?"

She nodded and stepped back. Surely *something* had sparked between her and Nash to bring them together. She thought back to their early days of dating, over six months ago. It had been exciting and fun. They'd easily become friends and then more after a few weeks. She liked talking to him, spending time with him, and he fit in with her long-term goals: stay in Little River forever. They hadn't spoken about the future specifically yet, but the transition would be an easy one. She knew it.

"What's wrong?" He stepped away from the table, where she noticed Styrofoam take-out boxes from the taco truck that came to town twice a week. He followed her into the living room, perching on the edge of the couch and waiting for her to sit down next to him. When she did, he put his arm over the top of the couch, his eyes pinched with worry.

"I need to be very honest with you, about us. About Tag."

Nash grimaced and reached one hand to take hers. "I overreacted today. Having him come back to town, knowing there was some history, and knowing that he meant to try and win you back got into my head. Obviously with him trying stuff, you'd want to avoid him and that doesn't have to mean anything."

She shook her head and pulled her hand away. "It's not that. Something's wrong with us, Nash. I'm not sure how I missed it."

He narrowed his eyes in suspicion as he studied her. "What do you mean?"

It wasn't a surprise that he had probably guessed how much of this had to do with Tag, with the way he made her feel. Maybe Nash felt like he'd overreacted, but at least he saw what the signs had meant. The way she wouldn't let any piece of Tag into her life at all could only mean she was afraid of what would happen if she did.

Heat rushed into her cheeks as she remembered that brief moment at the trailhead. Then others, the way her fingers had brushed his shirt when they argued the night he came back to Little River. It had startled her how much she wanted to grip his shirt and lean against him again. But she'd foolishly dismissed it, not caring to peer too deep into what it might mean. To pretend like he hadn't ignored her for eight years or that he hadn't ruined everything by asking her to do the impossible and then leaving her when she said no.

She turned to Nash though, grasping at some kind of straw that maybe Tag had just muddied up her brain and if she got out of here for a while, ignored him some more, things would fall back into place with Nash.

"When you kiss me, when we're together, when we're apart—what do you feel?" Now she took his hand in hers, weaving their fingers together so maybe she could demonstrate how there wasn't the emotion that there should be.

His head snapped back in surprise, proving he'd expected her to admit to her feelings for Tag. "I want to be with you, of course."

"Like in a so-distracting way that you can't really work? That I'm on your mind all the time? Like you rush out here after work because you can't wait another second?" she pressed.

He chewed on his lip as he listened, maybe the truth dawning on him for the first time too. "That's a first-dating sort of thing." But his tone held the questioning that Roxy had done herself since talking to Bellamy. The hope that she was wrong.

"Did you feel that then?" she asked.

He stared at her.

"Don't you want the kind of love where you still feel that way?"

He drew in a breath and pulled away from her, scooting to the arm of the couch. "But this is about Tag. About how you feel about him."

"Maybe," she admitted. "So hopefully when he's gone, I can figure out my life better, but I had to tell you." She rubbed her fingers over the microfiber of her couch, avoiding looking back up at Nash.

Accusation flowed through his voice, maybe not totally directed at her, but enough. "He grew up here too—with you. He is always going to be a part of your life," Nash said.

She looked up in time to see him run a hand through his hair and stand up.

She shook her head. "This is the first time in eight years Tag has come home. He told me a long time ago that he wasn't going to stay in Little River, and that's never changed." She grimaced at him, biting her lip. "I'm sorry."

"What does all this mean? I don't feel like you're about to run off with Tag, so you don't need my blessing for that..." Nash spread out his hands, confusion evident in his expression.

"It means that ... we need to take a break until I can understand if Tag is what's wrong right now or if there's something else I need to do to fix this." She waved her fingers between them. "I'm sorry," she said again for good measure.

After several silent moments, Nash came forward, leaning over to kiss her cheek. "I think we have something good, Rox. But I'll trust you here." He didn't wait for her to respond before he left the house.

CHAPTER TWELVE

E very day that went by that Tag didn't see Roxy stretched his ability to play this cool. The few days after they'd hiked, writing two new songs had consumed him. But then her absence started picking him apart. How had she gone from agreeing to hike with him to avoidance again?

He hated to admit that he struggled to find the right words for the last verse of the second song he'd started. He figured his moments with Roxy would be good for months' worth of songwriting, but it seemed that basking in her actual presence made him more in need of a fix. After sitting and staring at his notebook for a solid hour and only writing down the line *the sunrise makes your hair turn gold*, he headed downstairs in hopes of finding Roxy.

He found Bellamy instead, coming up to ask if he wanted lunch in his room again or if he wanted to eat with the rest of the guests.

"Does that include Roxy?" he asked.

Bellamy kept smiling, but the corners of her lips stiffened, the first indicator that something was indeed up. "She warned you that she didn't work down here a lot."

Tag studied Bellamy. "Thought she was trying to prove to her boyfriend that we're just friends, and now she's avoiding me again?"

Bellamy let out a breathy half-laugh. "Wow, there really isn't a line you won't cross when it comes to her, is there?"

He shrugged, not embarrassed about admitting to his eavesdropping. "I haven't found one yet."

This time Bellamy studied Tag with a soft *hmm*. "She's my best friend, and even if I believe she's ignoring something big, I can't be on your side for this."

An ally! Tag recognized the indecision in Bellamy's gaze. He reached out to take her arm. "That's because you don't know the whole story, only what Roxy's told you."

Bellamy pulled away and shook her head. "Even if I did, I won't go behind her back to help you. If you want to convince Roxy you love her, you've got to do it."

"I will," he said as she turned to head back down the stairs. "Why is she avoiding me again? What's going on with her boyfriend?" Tag called after her.

Bellamy ignored him, then stopped and turned back toward him. "You never said where you were having lunch."

He wasn't getting any work done in his room and he held onto the chance that Roxy might show up. "With everyone else."

———————————————

"WE HAVE A PROBLEM."

Bellamy's voice ringing through her living room startled Roxy enough that she nearly sliced one of her fingers off. She laid aside the knife and turned around from the counter where she was chopping up veggies for a salad.

"Do you want me to guess? Because all of my suspicions will have to do with Tag and why didn't we just say no in the first place?"

"Savannah just called me to ask if they could come over tomorrow morning and talk about where they want to set things up for this weekend." Bellamy placed two hands dramatically on the island.

Even though it had been a full five days since she'd hiked with Tag, Roxy's first thought was that she'd have to spend time up at the Ranch

House with Savannah in the morning and probably risk seeing him. "The wedding," she moaned when the real reason for Bellamy's concern dawned on her. "We'll have to talk to Beau. We can't move Savannah's wedding, unless we can convince her to use the cabin over at the Double A."

Bellamy shook her head. "Honeymooners are checking in this weekend."

Roxy blew out a breath. "This ranch is twenty square miles. Surely we can throw a wedding without giving away the fact that we're hiding Taggart Dubois up here."

"Every spot she mentioned going over this morning was on the Ranch House grounds. And you can't try and convince her otherwise for Tag's sake. This is her wedding!"

Roxy rubbed at her temples. "I know. You're right. Talk to Beau, explain the situation. I'm sure everyone will understand and Tag will just have to hide in his room for the afternoon. Is he still stuck in song-writing land?" she asked hopefully.

"Not really."

Roxy let loose another sigh. "Too bad. If he wants to keep things quiet, he'll just have to stay in his room for the afternoon or stay away somewhere else. We have plenty of things for him to do."

Bellamy leaned over the counter. "Have you talked to him since you broke up with Nash?"

"No," Roxy said automatically. "Why would I?"

Bellamy straightened and shrugged. "I think he'd be interested to know."

"That's exactly why I'm not going to tell him." Roxy picked the knife back up and finished chopping up her veggies. "But I will go over and talk to him about Savannah's wedding. In case he needs to smooth things over with Beau, it will be nice to have him on our side."

Bellamy tapped her fingers on the island and then moved to leave. "Okay." Her voice held all the opinions Roxy knew her friend held back about her approach to Tag, but Bellamy couldn't understand. She hadn't had her life turned upside down when Tag had claimed he'd loved her for years. She hadn't had to dissect love songs wondering if she'd missed something or if it was all for show, like she'd always thought. His declaration at his concert in July had certainly made interest in his new album skyrocket as everyone speculated whether heartbreak or happily ever after would inspire it after the drama they'd witnessed. He'd seemed genuine in every encounter she'd had with him since he arrived at the Ranch House, but living his life singing about over-the-top love stories might be influencing that more than she knew.

Never mind the fact that Roxy couldn't live her life on the road; it was too much to give up. She loved her home and the town needed her. And Tag couldn't come home to the ranch either. He was meant for bigger things. She and Tag both needed to come to terms with the fact that they weren't meant for each other.

"You'll plan on tomorrow morning too?" Bellamy asked. "Savannah's going to want you to walk over the grounds with her, not me."

"Yep." Roxy grinned over at Bellamy, setting aside her reluctance so her friend wouldn't push her to admit too much about Tag.

Bellamy sighed again and waved, disappearing back through the front door.

Roxy made her way over to the Ranch House after she'd had lunch. The last few years, the fall weather in Little River had stayed warmer than normal, and today wasn't an exception. With the temperature in the low seventies, Roxy donned a hoodie for her walk over.

"He went on a ride," Bellamy reported when Roxy came in the back door.

Roxy moved to walk down the hall to the main living area. "I'll wait here then."

"Why don't you saddle up and go find him? He said he was going to ride the creek. Easy to find." Bellamy wiggled her eyebrows.

"I don't like to ride horses."

"You've been holed up in your house for days." Bellamy took her arm and walked her out the back door.

"I went on a hike with Tag just a few days ago." Roxy pulled back and scowled.

"Nearly a week."

"Five days."

Bellamy raised her eyebrows. "Be a good host, Roxy. You'd do this for any other guest. Why are you avoiding Tag?" she finished with a way too innocent voice.

The bad news was that Bellamy had her there. Though she didn't particularly enjoy horseback riding, guests liked having a family member take them out. "That's not why you're pushing me," she protested. She shook loose of Bellamy's arm and reached down to slip off her nice booties and grab Bellamy's cowboy boots next to the door. "But it's not a big deal," she retorted as she stalked out the door.

She took her time saddling up one of the guest horses. Her dad had always thought it was sacrilegious that Roxy didn't own her own horse when she ran one of the biggest ranches in Wyoming for her family. She'd pointed out numerous times to him that she did most of that from an office, that her role wasn't like his had been, or his grandfather's, or any of his ancestors in the past seven generations. Danny took care of all of the day-to-day work, not her. And she preferred to do any work out of doors from one of the side-by-sides or her truck. When Dad had gotten sick, he'd made her promise to buy a horse. She'd joked with him that he was taking advantage but promised anyway. In the last couple of years, she still hadn't gotten around to it, maybe because it would mean really admitting that he was gone.

"What would Dad say about Tag?" she said in a soft sing-song voice as she led the horse to a mounting stool. She'd always gone to her mother and sisters for advice on love and her dad had never been one to offer unsolicited advice. Maybe Roxy should've thought to ask.

Like Bellamy had guessed, Tag wasn't hard to find. Roxy spotted him just a few miles from the Ranch House, letting his horse walk at a slow gait along the creek. She didn't rush to him, instead watching him while she approached. He wore a flannel shirt and a vest. No cowboy hat—she'd always teased him about that. *What self-respecting country star doesn't wear a cowboy hat?*

"Carrie Underwood," he'd shot back. Roxy had googled pictures of her

wearing one just for him. He'd taped a couple in his locker, but he insisted his UW baseball hat would be his trademark.

She'd bet he was wearing boots though. He turned as she got closer, and she caught sight of several days' worth of scruff on his face too. Her stupid heart skipped a few beats, especially when his face lit up with a grin.

"What is the occasion, Rox?" he asked, turning his horse to come meet her, as though she might disappear from his sight if he didn't make her stay. She couldn't blame him for that fear.

"Bellamy says I gotta treat you like a real guest. Something about you being famous or something." She smirked at him.

Tag's smile grew and he leaned forward in the saddle as he pulled his horse right up next to her, their legs brushing. "I don't want you to treat me like a guest," he said.

"In that case…" She turned the horse away, but he pulled back and cut her off.

"Stay," he said, tilting his head at her.

Funny, she thought, *that's all I wanted you to do eight years ago.* Stay and prove he meant his big words. "I do have some official business," she said instead, but she pulled her horse alongside his and they headed down the creek bed once again. She glanced down at Tag's feet to make sure he wore boots. They were even a bit worn, though the holes in his light wash jeans didn't look like the kind he'd worn in himself. "My cousin Savannah is getting married on Saturday," she said, forcing her thoughts away from Tag's good looks.

"You need a date?" he asked.

Actually … she did. She'd forgotten about that part of breaking up with Nash. Tag winked when she didn't answer right away and Roxy bit back a laugh. "She's getting married out here. I'm sorry, it's not on the official books because we're not charging her, obviously, so both Bellamy and I forgot." His brow furrowed in confusion. "You're going to have to make yourself scarce unless you want everyone to know you're out here," she explained.

"Oh. Yeah." He chuckled and turned back to stare at the scenery in front of them. "Being here like this ... it makes me forget that I'm not just home for some visit."

"You show up in Instagram posts from Savannah's wedding, there'll be enough teenage girls here to remind you," Roxy teased.

He cast her a look that made her shiver to the tips of her toes. How could he do that? Not even be close, not even touch her, but make her aware of every beat of her heart and the way she ached to be riding behind him, her arms wrapped around his waist. The ache had never really gone away after he first left.

"There are a few grown women who scream at my concerts too," he said.

"Ha." She pretended to scoff, but as closely as he studied her, he had to see the tell-tale pink in her cheeks judging by the way they flamed. His answer was a smile. Tag had always been able to read her mind and see into her heart.

He hummed something to himself and turned away. "I don't mind staying out of sight," he said. "And thanks for this ride. It means I'll have something to work on."

He didn't need to turn for her to catch his smile. "Oh, stop it," she muttered, but his hums just turned to whistles. Maybe if she'd listened to more of his songs, she could counter his insistence that he wrote them all about her. Surely there had to be a song about a truck or a dog in the mix somewhere. But he'd never been a dog person and she had no idea what kind of car he drove these days.

I HAVE WAITED for way too long for you to explain about you and Tag hiking together. I thought you had a strict boycott on anything to do with that boy.

Roxy couldn't help laughing a little at Taylor's text. She set aside the book she'd been reading while lounging on her couch and sent a text back. *Nash got worried about how we couldn't be friends, so I was trying to be friends again.*

And?

Roxy laughed again. She could almost picture her sister's impatient glare, maybe even tapping her fingers along the edge of her counter or on the floor next to her while she played with Tucker. *And what?*

And how did that work out?

Warmth immediately started spreading through Roxy when she remembered standing there at the truck with Tag inches away and she slid into a daydream where he had closed the space, pressed her up against the truck and showed her exactly what she'd been missing since he'd left. She drew in a long breath and shook her head. She could *not* get lost in all of that. It made making rational decisions really difficult.

Nash and I broke up, so there's that.

Her phone immediately began ringing. She sighed and picked up the phone, prepared to face some more uncomfortable truths about her feelings for Tag. Taylor was bound to drag them out of her.

"What the heck, Rox?" Taylor demanded. "What happened on that hike?"

Roxy sighed again. "Nothing, really. He just … made me realize I've been burying some stuff and it's not fair to Nash to keep going on like everything's okay. Not until I get Tag out of my system."

Taylor hesitated before replying, "And that's what you want? Getting Tag out of your system?"

"We've been over and over this, T. How can I even know if any of it's real?"

Taylor scoffed. "By seeing what happens."

"It's pointless. We don't want the same life. There's no future, no matter what I want now."

"What exactly *do* you want now?" Taylor's voice turned light with teasing and suggestion, making Roxy laugh, but also bringing back that image of her and Tag wrapped up in each other's arms.

"Oh, girl…" She said letting out a long breath. "Between you and me—and if you breathe a word of this to Bellamy, I swear I will come and steal every article of clothing in your closet—I wouldn't mind letting that boy kiss me until I couldn't think straight." She thought of how he'd looked on that horse today, like he definitely could belong on this ranch. It made her heart a bit desperate.

Taylor lowered her voice. "I mean, between you and me," she teased. "They didn't vote him Country Music's Sexiest Star for nothing..." She whistled.

"Amen," Roxy said with a resigned laugh. "Amen."

CHAPTER THIRTEEN

Roxy leaned against a pillar on the back porch and stared out at the back garden. It hadn't been a surprise to her when Savannah had come right out here when she came to decide on locations and said this was the spot.

"We can do the main room inside if the weather turns bad," she'd said, "but the forecast says seventy."

And the weather had held out, an added blessing on the day. The sun would set soon and a chill would chase the guests inside. Bellamy and Roxy had gathered up as many employees who'd already signed the nondisclosure contracts to help out, and when it came time, they'd pick up the party and arrange everything between the big dining and living area. It wasn't the way the Ranch House usually did weddings, at least the handful they'd done since opening, but Savannah had insisted she liked the casual atmosphere better anyway.

For now, Roxy pulled the long cardigan tighter around her and grinned at the twinkling lights, the planked dancing floor, and the scent of roses wafting around them.

"Have I mentioned enough yet how grateful I am that we could get married here?" Savannah came up behind Roxy and put an arm around her shoulders.

"Stop, Savannah. There was never any question that a great-granddaughter of Ed Pender had the right." She reached around her cousin's waist to hug her back.

"Thank you anyway. From the bottom of my heart. It's beautiful and perfect, and I feel very connected to the roots of this ranch." They leaned their heads together and stared out at the garden for a few moments of silence. "I heard you had someone stashed away up here—like a big deal celebrity," Savannah said, pulling away to eye Roxy expectantly. "Like maybe Tag Turner." She wiggled her eyebrows.

The blood drained from Roxy's face. Nash wouldn't have said something, would he? But how else would anyone in town know? Tag had kept to himself when Savannah had come a few days earlier, and she hadn't seen hide nor hair of him since they'd started setting up.

"You can't say a word, Savannah," she admonished. "We have a contract—"

Savannah held up a hand and pointed past her. "Then that boy isn't abiding by it himself."

Roxy swiveled around to see Tag coming up the cobbled walkway toward them, dressed in a sharp gray suit and dark blue tie. She pulled in a long breath, telling herself that the fact that her heart had sped up had to do with worrying about people finding out about him being at the Arrow C, and not the way he stared at her as he strode toward her.

"Congratulations, Savannah," he said when he met them. He put a hand on Savannah's back and leaned over to kiss her cheek.

"Nice of you to drop by." She raised her eyebrows as he pulled away.

"Why wouldn't I? I'm practically family." He put his hands in his pockets, rocking backward and placing himself right next to Roxy. She noted that he no longer wore that cheap cologne he'd always used in high school, but she liked the sharp scent of whatever he wore now. And the money he must have spent on the custom suit. Boy…

"You wish," Savannah said, laughing and shaking her head at Tag, and a good thing, because Roxy had been about to fall into a dangerous spell.

Tag laughed with Savannah and glanced over at Roxy before turning back to Savannah. "Got any requests?" he asked.

Savannah's mouth dropped open. "Tag Turner, are you serious?" she asked, bouncing on her toes with glee. "You're gonna sing at my wedding?"

"Might as well, since I'm here."

Roxy caught herself leaning into him and straightened. The suit and the cologne were a one-two punch, but his grin as he watched Savannah's excitement threatened to KO Roxy. She barely heard the names of the songs her cousin rattled off and the multiple thank you's mixed in there.

"And when I'm done," Tag said, bringing Roxy back to the present yet again, "Can I have a dance with you?"

"I can't," Roxy breathed, chewing on her lip when Tag's face fell. "Everyone will see."

"You've always been embarrassed of me, but I'd hoped that my stardom had taken care of all that."

"Stop it." She couldn't help laughing at him, and the disappointment flitted out of his expression. "Everyone here will take pictures and post them everywhere—and it's you, so it will all get blown out of proportion. And I just broke up with Nash, so that's the last thing he needs to see on everyone's feed."

"You broke up with Nash?" Tag's eyebrows shot up, and if she hadn't been so irritated with herself that she'd admitted that particular bit, she might have laughed at the way that sympathy battled on his face with his excitement.

"Yes. No, not really. It's more of a break. Until you leave town." His eyebrows shot even higher, and Roxy scowled. "Not like that. You've purposefully been making things complicated, Tag, and you know it."

He scowled. "He broke up with you because of what I did at the concert and me being here?" The scowl deepened with protectiveness that made Roxy's mind spin. "The hike? Did he think something happened when we went on that hike?"

Something *had* happened, but Roxy shook her head. "No. You muddy up things in me and that wasn't fair to him."

The excitement won out again as a smile threatened on Tag's lips, though guilt tugged at the edges. Lips she lingered over looking at for longer than she should. "You broke up with him?" he guessed.

"We took a break," she corrected, but that felt like a lie. "Go sing for Savannah. Everyone's waiting." She pushed him away, and he obliged, but he cast more than one look back at her as he made his way to the stage. Winnie appeared from the crowd and handed him a guitar.

People had been whispering and chattering his name since he'd shown up, but that all immediately died down when he stepped up to the microphone. It was a strange thing to see him behind that instrument in a suit and not his usual jeans and flannel shirt or t-shirt. He didn't look like Taggart Dubois, even though the band started playing one of his songs.

Tag Turner had come home this time.

"I missed you all," he said, to laughter and applause. "So I figured I'd drop back in to town and crash Savannah and Tanner's party. You all mind?"

Everyone shouted "No!" and cheered some more. Roxy dropped onto the porch step and leaned her elbows on her knees, resting her head in her hands as she watched him. As soon as he started the first song, one she'd never heard that had quite a few mentions of trucks and one reference to a dog, his gaze found hers, like it always had before when he sang.

Her heart clenched. Another reason she'd avoided his concerts. Listening to his smooth voice float through the air like it was only for her stirred in her the need for Tag that she'd struggled to tamp down after Laramie. The what-if-he's-serious mixing with maybe-I've-always-loved-him-too.

He finished that one, pulling his gaze away to make fun of Savannah's choice of song for a wedding and said he had one he thought might be better for the occasion. He started playing one that made Roxy's lips quirk into a smile. He was changing the lyrics of a song he'd written in high school, inserting Savanna and Tanner's names. They swayed slowly on the dance floor together as everyone else watched, but still Tag's eyes were for Roxy, even when everyone else watched the happy couple or Tag.

So many people among the guests tonight had been there the first time Tag sang this song, listening to his honeyed voice and falling in love with him. Roxy remembered watching the way his girlfriend leaned in toward him, her eyes saying she believed this song was for her.

But Tag had sung to Roxy, like always. Tag always sang to Roxy, so though they'd never officially dated, she could see why people in town would call her Tag's sweetheart, even considering the string of girl-friends he'd had.

That girl didn't last long. Roxy had lectured Tag about that later that night, telling him he was breaking that girl's heart just because he insisted on singing to Roxy. "You're my reason, darlin'," he'd said in a fake country drawl, but then more seriously, "That would be a lie, Rox. I don't lie with my music." Sixteen-year-old Roxy hadn't under-stood the depth of that. She'd rolled her eyes and asked him to be seri-ous, just for once. He'd turned away and stared down at his guitar for a long time. Eighteen-year-old Roxy hadn't understood either. Twenty-six-year-old Roxy was only just coming to.

He played a few more songs before he left the stage to a standing ovation. Savannah and Tanner hurried up to him when he stepped down, both of them thanking him. She didn't know how he'd make people think he'd left the Ranch House after tonight, but by the look of contentment on his face, it had been worth it for him.

When he met her gaze amid the people who gathered around to talk to him, Roxy questioned if she'd ever be able to keep from believing it all could be some fairy-tale come true. That Tag Turner did really love her. That he *still* loved her. That they could believe that magic forever.

<hr>

A FEW PEOPLE from town made their way out to the ranch in the days after the wedding, but Tag would disappear and Bellamy would assure them that he'd left the morning after the wedding. Word must have started to get around town, because she hadn't heard of any more curious onlookers in a couple of days and the only mentions of the event on social media had talked about Tag stopping by his hometown for a friend's wedding, with, of course, some speculation about whether or not he'd made another play for his old sweetheart Roxy Adams. Celebrity gossip sites had scrutinized the pictures taken at the wedding, pointing out Roxy's presence there.

With the wedding over and any preparations that had to be made over at the Ranch House finished, Roxy kept herself away. Listening to him play had made it difficult to stay off the road that would lead to a broken heart when Tag left again. She was starting to believe that he did love her, but they faced too many obstacles—like the fact that they lived two very different lives. But she struggled to distract herself.

If any other guests were staying at the Ranch House, she would have gone down and wallowed with Bellamy, discussing whether or not she'd made the right choice with Nash, and drowned her worries in something delicious that Bellamy had made.

Since it was after dinner time, Bellamy was probably in the apartment at the Ranch House. Another one of the renovations they'd made was cutting off the large master suite from the guest area and adding a small kitchenette, allowing the manager to live on site.

Roxy could sneak over to the Ranch House to hang out with Bellamy, and it would be far more distracting than the current Netflix binge she'd fallen into. She clicked the button on her phone to light it up and opened her message app to text Bellamy. A text from earlier that day with a link to something on Facebook popped up. *Have you seen this?* Bellamy had messaged.

Roxy clicked it, then tensed when she saw it was a video from Tag, the YouTube video of Roxy's Song. She almost clicked out when she noticed a comment thread underneath that she hadn't seen the first time she commented on the video. *This isn't the same song as before. They changed it!* Followed by some angry emojis. Other people replied to the thread along the same lines, making the claim that the lyrics of the first verse had changed.

Intrigued, Roxy pressed play on the video, noting right away that Tag recorded from a home recording studio, like before, but the room you could see behind him had changed. He'd recorded this version at the Ranch House.

She steeled herself against the way his smooth voice could hypnotize her and focused on the supposed new lyrics—her heart softening as she listened. The lines about the girl with honey-colored curls had disappeared. Instead, Tag sang about the mountains he missed, familiar roads with memories, and dusty boots by the door.

She paused the video and sat back against her couch. In reality, the damage had already been done when he sang that song at the concert in front of pretty much everyone in Little River. Not to mention the declaration and the ad-libbed lyrics at the end. But this change still softened her heart. That first verse had been the reason most people loved the song—for locals, the connection they'd seen to his history in his hometown; for others, the romantic theme of the girl next door. If Tag recorded this version on his album, it would suffer. Maybe not noticeably, considering his popularity, but it would still affect it.

And to her surprise, she found herself missing the original lyrics. The ones that had reminded her so forcibly of the boy she lost that she had to run away from those feelings catching up with her.

She pocketed her phone, put on a jacket, and left her house, headed for the Ranch House to discuss this with Bellamy. She heard the strains of the guitar as soon as she set foot outside and nearly turned back in. But his music pulled her, and she didn't want to resist it.

Fire flickered from the pit at the back of the Ranch House, and as she approached, she made out the shapes of five people sitting around it on the benches. It had been another warm September day, but the night air chilled around them, propelling Roxy to the fire. At least she told herself that.

Tag glanced her direction when she slipped into a seat next to Bellamy, smiling and holding her gaze but never missing a beat in the song he played, an old one of his from before she stopped listening to his music.

"Don't you think his people get sick of hearing him all the time," she joked in a quiet voice to Bellamy, hoping to distract herself from the way Tag kept staring at her. It had been one thing among the fifty plus guests at the wedding, another in this more intimate setting.

Bellamy granted her a smile but raised her eyebrows in a way that made Roxy aware that her friend saw right through her. "Winnie was playing before. Beau and Quinn finally got Tag to play. This was Quinn's request."

"It's a good song," Roxy murmured, turning back to gaze at Tag again. That fire that threatened to overtake her at the top of the trailhead settled into a simmer in her chest, glowing warmer and warmer. As he played the last strains, Quinn begged for one of his new ones. Tag shook his head, instead starting another old one, but Quinn didn't give up, protesting over Tag's voice until he gave in.

Bellamy squeezed Roxy's leg. "This is it, Rox," she whispered, leaning in to listen just like all the girls who fell a little in love with Tag did. Roxy had always been able to see why. Now that she was really listening to him, it was difficult to understand why she hadn't seen more in his songs before now. Sure, he'd always said she was his muse, but that just meant inspiration, not literal descriptions of his feelings for her, right? At least, that's what she'd been telling herself for a long time.

The fire rose inside her, his words adding fuel to the flame, the way he held her gaze like pouring on gasoline. The words swirled inside her and created the picture he sang about a lifetime together. Thank heavens he hadn't sang this at the wedding. She definitely would have made a scene.

She stopped her train of thought when that lifetime came to a vision of Tag, sprawled out across her couch and her curled up next to him.

That wasn't real, no matter how much she wished it. He might be genuine, but he wasn't being practical.

None of his dreams about their future would ever be real. Tag's life was too big for that.

She blinked, looking around her in surprise to notice that only she and Tag sat outside next to the fire.

"Well, this is awkward," she said staring at her hands.

He chuckled, easy as ever. "No, it's not, Rox." He kept on strumming, only humming now, as he stood and made his way over to her. He sat in the spot Bellamy had vacated. When she glanced in the house, she caught sight of the others in the dining room, all gathered around the table in conversation, a window open to let in the music.

"You have to stop singing those songs," she said, pleading with him.

"Never." His answer held the fierceness that it always had when she questioned his musical declarations of love.

"Nothing's changed. We both want different things." Never mind the fire. Never mind the ache. Giving in would mean falling into that pit of hurt he'd left behind before.

"I just want you." He sang those words and then nodded to himself, his smile growing wider. "I just need you, Rox."

"Are you staying this time?" she asked.

He didn't answer and for the first time that she'd noticed since she walked up to the fire pit, he dropped his gaze to his guitar. So they sat like that for several minutes, Tag playing with the occasional hum.

"Thank you," she said when she broke the silence. "For Roxy's Song, for changing it."

"I never meant to hurt you." Still he stared down at his guitar. The irony was that it hurt her to recognize that insisting that he temper his feelings by changing those lyrics had hurt him.

"I know. That's why you should sing the original on the album."

His gaze snapped up. "Really?"

He wanted more from her in that moment than she could say. "People really liked it." Even as she said the words, she wished she'd been silent.

His gaze dropped back to the guitar. "People like real." He quit playing and set his guitar aside. "And every song about love I've ever sung? That was real. That was about you. You are the reason I'm famous."

She took her hands in his and leaned over them, resting her cheeks against them. *Please stay home*, her heart begged. Now that she recog-

nized what she'd given up before, it was all that stood between them—
the life she needed.

The life she couldn't ask Tag to give her. To give up his very soul.
Singing to her on a couch at night and lullabies (oh, her heart gasped
at that thought) would never be enough.

She stood up, and he watched her, confusion in the way his
eyebrows slanted, desperation in the way he gripped her hands. "I
really like that new song," she said. She pulled away from him and
headed back down the road. That was the closest she would ever
come to asking Tag to give it all up to love her.

CHAPTER FOURTEEN

Beau insisted that Tag leave the Ranch House the next day. They donned helmets and signed out one of the side-by-side ATVs the Arrow C owned. Beau grabbed a map of the trails they could drive in the area, but Tag knew them all by heart anyway. He'd grown up with Roxy riding around this ranch.

He let Beau drive. Tag's brain was hung up on the new song he'd written and the ideas for the future he'd purposefully conjured to bring that song to life. He'd meant to win her back with Roxy's Song, but when he'd started this new one, he'd realized this was the one that would speak to Roxy's heart. Hearing her say she liked it solidified his desperation to make that future come true.

What surprised him was that every time he brought those daydreams to mind, he didn't picture Roxy on his Tennessee farm outside of Nashville. He pictured them here. He hadn't seen the inside of Roxy's house, so those parts blurred, but he could see him throwing a football around in her front yard, and riding horses with a little girl in the saddle in front of him since Roxy didn't like riding. Sitting out on the swing he'd seen on her front porch and serenading her on summer nights.

When Beau pulled to the top of a lookout and cut the engine, both men removed their helmets and got out to admire the view. Most people only saw the beauty of these mountains from the highway that ran over the top. Tag had gotten the privilege of hiking, riding, and driving the many mountain roads that led to gorgeous vistas like the one he stared out over now—a green valley carpeted by pine trees as far as he could see.

He'd left it all, because as beautiful as it was, and he'd always recognized that, his dreams meant more. He had never understood why Roxy couldn't leave it for him.

"Am I too young to retire?" he asked Beau.

Beau's head snapped in his direction, but one thing that Tag liked about his manager was the fact that he took time to consider the things he said in situations like this. After about thirty seconds he asked, "Would she be worth it?"

"Without a doubt." Tag stared across the valley. "Everything I've done up to this point, the awards I've won, none of it is enough without her. Nothing will be enough. I could go on to be the next George Strait and my life wouldn't be complete." All this time, he'd thought Roxy was running away from him, but maybe all this time he'd been running away from her. Maybe his dreams weren't as important as he thought, like Roxy had tried to tell him all along.

Silence settled between them for a long time before Beau sighed. "You really could be the next George Strait," he said in a low voice.

Tag chuckled. "I did all the things I set out to do. That's no small accomplishment."

Beau reached over from where they both leaned against the front of the ATV and clapped Tag on the shoulder. "That's the truth."

They left the discussion at that as they headed back for the Ranch House. Having said it out loud, made the offer, even if not to Roxy yet, made him consider how he'd always approached winning her over. He'd expected her to eventually see his side. His dreams, his accomplishments were a big deal. Roxy's wishes to stay home in this small-town life seemed unreasonable in the face of all he'd done. Pure stubbornness.

But she loved the idea of home and family, settled here, as much as he loved his career, and he'd dismissed that for too long. He'd done a lot in the last eight years and it felt like ripping out a part of him to walk away, but Roxy could make up for more than what he'd leave behind.

✕———————————✕

WHEN THE SOUNDS of a guitar wafted in through her open living room window, Roxy immediately went to close out whatever impromptu concert Tag was giving over at the ranch house. The night before had worn down her resistance to him and any more of his new songs about a life with her might push her over the edge, make getting over him this time as bad as it had been back in college.

But as she stood next to the window, she realized the music came from much closer than she'd first guessed. Specifically, from her front porch.

She went to her front door and pulled it open. Tag grinned at her from where he sat on her porch swing. Oh, heaven help her, he looked like the boy she'd first fallen in love with—dirty jeans and boots, his hair matted against one side with sweat and dirt, and a t-shirt hanging just right over his broad shoulders. The slick cowboy that girls across the country sighed over could make Roxy's heart pitter-patter along with the rest of them, but this man? She had to grip the doorframe just to keep from fainting.

She recognized the song that Bellamy had told her about, the one he'd played last night to force her to picture their future. It took her a second, but she realized he'd changed the words to this song too. *"I'm gonna sit with Roxy on this porch swing. Watch our babies play in the yard. Live the life that she's always dreamed. Count my success in just being by her side."*

She held up a hand as she stepped out, begging him to stop. "You said you didn't lie with your music, Tag, but you know we can't have the things you're talking about."

Tag set his guitar aside and stood up. "We can if I choose you."

She stilled, shock dousing her at what he'd just offered. What she'd wanted him to offer all those years ago but had known it was unfair to ask. "You can't choose me," she whispered.

"I can. I'd choose you every day over this, Rox. Don't you know that? In any lifetime, any world, I'd choose you."

Curse him, he could wax poetic even without that blasted guitar in his hands. "You're talking nonsense," she insisted. She put a hand over her eyes, the weight of it all crashing over her. Tag leaving country music for her. Walking away at the top of his game. She had never considered him actually doing this. Maybe she'd even hid behind that every time she pushed him away. What would it cost him to give her what she needed?

"You're talking crazy," she muttered, panic inside her building. He would lose a part of him—and that would be her fault.

"Roxy..." His voice was gentle and soothing, and she loved and hated how he understood her fears without even knowing them.

"Why'd you come back?" she cried. "You can't just walk away! We both could've been happy apart, but you dragged us through this when what we want will never be the same."

He took a long stride to close the distance between them, his hands coming to her hips to pull her closer. "Were you happy without me, Rox?" he asked in a low, husky voice. He moved in, trapping her between him and the door, a situation that both terrified her and made an ache for him sear her.

The fire roared through her as he bent over her, pressing his lips to hers. It was all far better than she remembered, maybe because eight years of memories over their last kiss hadn't done this justice. She wrapped her arms around him, pulling him to her tighter, tighter even than he held her, as though she could make up for lost time in this one embrace. She gripped his shoulders—that and his arms felt like the only thing keeping her standing. His hands ran up her back, leaving another streak of fire there. Those lips—the sweet lips that sang only to her—pressed a different song into her now, one that reminded her of slow, heady tunes and crashing beats all at the same time.

He pulled back for a ragged breath, staring at her with desperation, and whispering her name in a way that made her stomach tumble and throw herself back to him. He lifted her to her tip toes as he kissed her again and she wrapped her arms around his neck, need for him shooting through her like lightning bolts. She pictured kissing him like this all the time, there on the porch, sweet kisses together on the swing. She wanted to do that forever.

But they couldn't. Not really.

Forget that this kiss put to shame any kiss she'd ever shared with anyone. It was crazy to think they could have it all. That he wouldn't turn bitter in a year or two or beg to go back. And how could she tell him no after all he'd just offered?

She shoved away. "No. You can't do this." Then she shoved him harder, because no, she hadn't been happy without him, but she'd been fine. Now she wouldn't ever be again, and nothing had really changed. But the shoving only moved him an inch away, his face stiff with confusion and hurt. So she lashed out with words.

"You can't come here after all this time and make some big announcement that you still love me and expect things to just work out, Tag," she cried. He expected too much. He took too much. She needed too much.

He shook his head, frustration evident in the slant of his brows and the stiff way he stepped back. "I never stopped telling you I loved you, Roxy," he said. "I've been singing it for eight years. I sent you tickets to every concert I ever played, hoping you'd show up. I didn't just walk away like you did."

"You stopped sending tickets years ago." Emotion blocked her chest as she remembered getting those envelopes in the first months after he left her in Laramie. Of thinking she'd finally gotten through the worst of missing him, only to see the notes begging her to come.

His scowl deepened, the fire between them turning his eyes dark with anger. "Every concert, Roxy. Every. Single. One. And you never showed up. Not once."

She clenched her fists against this new accusation. He'd probably trusted it to some assistant, living his big life. "You're saying you'll stay in this moment because you can't be sensible about our future. You'll choose me now even if all it does is make us both miserable in the end." That's the path this had always led to. Both of them forcing fate and not understanding the consequences. She'd been smart to try and take the path the first time he'd tried sweeping her off her feet. If only he'd listened.

He took another step away and then another, glaring at her as he retreated across the porch. "I'd forgotten how hard it was to make you happy," he snapped, the words whipping across her as though he'd used his hand. "You hate me because I left. You hate me when I beg to stay. You're just looking for a reason not to love me." He stalked off the porch, grabbing his guitar on the way. When he got to the bottom, he whirled on her. "All I've ever done is pour my heart out to you, with every word, with every song. You never understood any of it, and I never got it until now that you've never tried. That you don't even want to."

He marched the rest of the way out of the yard without looking back, hopping into a side-by-side ATV parked in her driveway and then speeding away, pebbles flying in his wake.

Roxy could shut out his songs until her dying day, never listen to another one, but she couldn't unhear the one he'd sung on her porch only a few moments ago. Or unhear the song he'd brought back to life inside her with his kiss. Or shut off the haunting melody his pain and his anger played inside her.

When he'd walked out the door in Laramie, the weight of losing him had taken away her breath. She'd felt deep inside that it had changed something for them that she could never fix. It had felt like the last goodbye. But this one? It felt as though he'd snatched away her entire life.

BY THE NEXT MORNING, Tag and his entourage had left Little River. Roxy watched two SUVs, black like the ones that had brought him a month before, roll down the county road to the highway, dust kicking up behind them. When he'd first shown up, she had expected his finally leaving to bring with it a sense of relief, of release. Another encounter with Tag survived.

But the sight of those SUVs turning onto the highway and disappearing from sight only left her with emptiness.

CHAPTER FIFTEEN

That evening, Roxy trudged down the road to the Ranch House. She cringed when she opened the front door and no sounds of music drifted down to her. Funny how after just a few weeks, that had become the normal. And it pricked at her heart when she realized she missed it. Maybe she had been missing it all this time. Her thoughts went to that picture Tag had created of him playing just for her the rest of his life. Having his music back had reminded her that a piece of her heart had always expected to hear him play every day for the rest of her life. She quickly dismissed those thoughts. Dwelling on them the last day and a half had exhausted her.

Bellamy wasn't in her office, so Roxy went upstairs, avoiding looking at the closed door of her old room, avoiding stepping inside to catch the lingering scent of Tag's cologne or deodorant or him. To search for anything he might have left behind.

She tapped on the door to the manager's apartment, studying the small wooden sign that labeled the room as "Private" while she waited for Bellamy to answer.

"Hey," Bellamy said when she pulled the door open. She reached over and gave Roxy a hug before ushering her inside. This room had belonged to Roxy's parents. Their large, king bed had rested right in the center of the far wall against the big windows. In the space where her mother had decorated with a sofa and chaise was a kitchenette with a small, round table and two chairs off to the side. Bellamy had a much smaller bed in the space to make room for two loveseats in another corner.

Roxy sat on the edge of Bellamy's bed, much the way she would've sat on her mom's when Roxy was in high school, and turned to her friend. "I'm sorry I messed it all up."

Bellamy scowled for a moment and then waved the words away. "They paid through the end of the month, which is a week longer than we thought they'd stay, to be honest. He originally asked for three weeks. Plus, Tag took a picture with me in front of the house before he left and told me to make sure we let people know he'd stayed there. Then he did this—" She pulled out her phone to show Roxy a picture taken of the Ranch House, with the mountains in the back ground and the miles of open plains surrounding it. He must have snapped it as they drove away. It was posted to Tag's Instagram feed, praising the peace and quiet he'd enjoyed while finishing up his album. *It will be the best one yet*, the caption promised. She pulled in a short breath and then looked away.

"So don't apologize to me," Bellamy went on, settling on the bed beside Roxy. "Because the bookings have been coming in like crazy all day, and I've even had a couple phone calls from people representing A-listers for quiet, out-of-the-way vacations with their families." Bellamy put a hand on Roxy's arm. "The only person you need to apologize to is yourself—and maybe Tag."

"To myself?" Roxy scowled and turned to look at Bellamy. "What's that supposed to mean?"

"For screwing something up so bad." Bellamy stood up and went to the fridge, opening the freezer on top and pulling out a pint of ice cream. She grabbed two spoons from one of the drawers and then came back to the bed, opening the top of the ice cream before offering it to Roxy.

"It might hurt now, but I did what was best for both of us," Roxy insisted, digging her spoon in. Bellamy scoffed, which deepened

Roxy's glare. "Eventually he'd want to go back, and then he'd get bitter about making a choice to leave all that behind. He's doing what he should be doing and I can't hold him back from that."

"So don't." Bellamy pointed her spoon at Roxy.

"I'm not raising my kids on the road. What kind of life is that for any of us? And I need to be in Little River for the ranch, and the Ranch House, and whatever comes in the future. I can't just walk away." Roxy flung out her hands in protest and nearly dropped a spoonful of ice cream onto the hardwood floor. She swung it back to her mouth just in time.

"So don't," Bellamy repeated.

It was Roxy's turn to scoff. "You're not making any sense. We can't have both; that's what's kept us apart this whole time."

"That was actually your stubbornness," Bellamy said. "Do you think I'm good at my job?"

Roxy blinked at the sudden change of topic. "You're fabulous at your job."

"So why do you think you have to be here twenty-four-seven so things don't fall apart?"

"I..." There was always paperwork to be done, guests to help with, events to help coordinate.

All things Bellamy could manage on her own, really.

"You can be here. And you can spend some time away. And this place will still be running, cross my heart. So you can quit ignoring the fact that Tag Turner has been serious about loving you since he was sixteen."

Roxy shoved the ice cream back at her friend. "This is tainted, isn't it? You shared it with Tag last night, it sounds like, and had the same heart-to-heart?"

Bellamy had the nerve to laugh. "Something like it, though I was probably a little more sympathetic."

Roxy gasped in indignation. "You're on his side!"

"Rox, your side is indefensible!" Bellamy said, earning another gasp. "You've been afraid all this time of what loving him meant, what it meant giving up for you, so you insist that he's the one leaving."

"Not falling for his charm just because he rides into town and makes these grand gestures is *not* illogical. Wanting my quiet life here on the ranch instead of some crazy traveling circus is also *not* illogical. Why can't he just accept that something will always be missing for us —him missing the road. Me missing home. Why set ourselves up for all that heartache?"

Bellamy sighed and stood up to put the ice cream on the table. "Tag said something to me last night, something I don't know if he got the chance to tell you. He said it wouldn't really matter what else he accomplished in life if he didn't have you. It made me think that he gets it—and you don't. What family are you going to raise without him, Rox?" she asked.

"Well, it might take some time getting over Tag once and for all, but I'm sure I can find *someone*," she snapped. She might have had something really good with Nash if Tag hadn't swept in and ruined it. Next time, she'd be sensible and stay away when he rolled back into town for peace and quiet. Not that he ever would again. She shoved away the jolt of pain that seared through her at that thought, instead stalking toward the door, angry that her friend had been charmed by Tag into believing the fairy tale he kept spouting.

"Wait, one second," Bellamy said, making Roxy turn to her before she flung open the door. "Is all this worth it? Is it worth losing him?"

Roxy took a deep breath, tears already starting. She kept insisting she could see the end, that she was saving them from the pain, but in the past couple of days, the misery she knew would come later had been blurred by the misery right now. "I don't know," she whispered.

Bellamy came over to the door and took Roxy's hands. "One more thing," she said, gripping her friend. "Just because he says it in song, don't ever doubt that that man loves you. You say he never showed you, but he's been saying it for eight years and you didn't notice. Every song he's written has you at the heart, so just listen."

———————

"CAN YOU SCHEDULE STUDIO TIME ASAP?" Tag asked Beau as they

headed past baggage claim at Nashville International and out into the night for their separate cars.

Beau raised an eyebrow, although Tag had pulled his cap so low that he almost didn't catch it. "You sure you want to jump right back in? We've got plenty of time for…" He waved his hands around, making Tag chuckle.

"Recovery? No, I don't need that. I've made a career out of my heartbreak for that girl. Why stop now?" From the corner of his eye, he saw a group of women snapping photos on their cell phones and he hurried his pace. One thing he didn't need tonight was to force a smile and be charming Taggart Dubois.

"If you're sure." Beau nodded and the two stepped out onto the sidewalk to catch their respective rides. A vaguely familiar driver with a "Taggart Dubois" sign stepped forward, but when he saw Tag, he swept the sign out of sight and opened a door to a silver sedan parked on the curb.

"One second," Tag said, calling back to Beau and Quinn's cab. Beau stepped away from the car door and met Tag as he walked back toward him. "Something's been bothering me since we left. Roxy said she hasn't gotten concert tickets for years. I kept trying to tell myself it was guilt talking, but—"

Beau held up a hand, then closed his eyes and sighed. "No. That one is on me." He glanced around them, squinting at the small handful of people coming and going in the late-night hour. "When she never came, and then when she sent back those tickets … You were so hurt. I don't know if you remember, but you stopped writing for a couple weeks after she sent them back. I'd never seen you *not* write, not even on your busiest days. You always at least wrote a line or two. I quit sending them so she couldn't send them back and hurt you like that some more. But I swear I did it as your friend, not as someone concerned with your career. Cross my heart, Tag."

Tag nodded. "It won't be like that now." He gave Beau a clap on the shoulder, reassuring him that he was forgiven. Tag didn't blame him. It had been a dark time when show after show would pass and she wouldn't come.

"Get some rest." Beau returned the shoulder pat and then turned and climbed inside the cab.

Quinn cast Tag a look before she followed suit, but she didn't say anything. Tag's crew had obviously guessed that his hasty departure from Little River, and his insistence that everyone leave as well, had meant something had gone down between him and Roxy, but he didn't want to discuss it with her. Quinn had grown to like Roxy as they worked out the details to whatever project Quinn was helping with. He couldn't bear to hear it if Quinn took Roxy's pragmatic view of things—that they'd been doomed all along—rather than see how Roxy had been the one to doom them.

When Tag settled into the back of the sedan, he slumped in the seat. He hadn't been able to sleep on any of the flights back to Nashville and it evaded him now too even though exhaustion wrapped around him. He kept picturing the anger in Roxy's expression, the pinch of her lips and the wrinkle between her eyebrows when she'd pulled away from him after their kiss. Only seconds before, her immediate response to that kiss had sent hope winging through him for the first time in a while. The way she'd gripped him had made him believe, for a few precious moments, that he'd done the right thing in giving everything up for her, never mind how he'd been seconds away from scooping her up into his arms and carrying her inside. For him, that kiss had made the earth move. Made him picture exactly what he'd sang to her: spending evenings sitting on that swing with her, watching their kids play in the yard, driving around to the far reaches of that ranch with a little boy in a matching baseball cap, taking his little girl on a picnic, convincing Roxy that a moonlit horseback ride along the creek could be romantic.

He had never once pictured that she would snatch it all back before the thoughts could even fully form. He'd spent the better part of loving Roxy Adams figuring out how to get over Roxy Adams, so it couldn't be too hard to get her out of his heart once and for all, could it? It was the only thing he could be certain of right now—that he was done trying to win her heart and prove his love.

That had sparked a fear in him that he'd been too distracted so far to really ponder on. Once he'd worked through the heartache, the anger, the frustration, once he'd peddled the last of the songs he could squeeze out of that hopeless relationship, what would be left for him to sing? One didn't just find a muse by heading down to the grocery store, which left him in a pickle. He could save himself from the pain of loving her anymore, but that meant making sure no piece of her remained.

And *that* meant firebombing his career.

He sighed. It couldn't be that bad. He had been angry and hurt and sad enough when she'd returned those tickets that the words seemed to flee. Eventually all that would go away and he'd find something new to write about. He was probably due an album with more songs about trucks and farms and all those other things except for love. He was making things feel hopeless right now in his mind because everything felt hopeless. He hummed a few bars to himself, bringing a smile that at least the last two days had sparked something new. Until he realized he was humming the song he'd sang for her on her porch swing.

He bit off a groan.

CHAPTER SIXTEEN

In eight years, Tag had put out four albums with an average of eleven songs apiece. That left Roxy with approximately three hours of music. Not all that much, she thought, when she first sat down with her phone.

Not all that much until she had to replay a good number of them so she could really *hear* the lyrics. She was locked away for the whole day, and by the time the last song on the last album had played, she'd graduated to watching every live video he'd posted on Facebook. Two days later, she was only halfway through and the whole exercise had messed up her emotions irrevocably. She had been much too pragmatic of a teenager, she decided. How had she not melted into a puddle at his feet whenever he held her gaze as he sang? Had she known, all along, that they couldn't have a happily ever after? Had she guarded her heart even then?

She was looking up Tag's previous tours, grimacing at his vigorous schedule, when her phone rang with a video call. Hope flitted through her heart that maybe Tag hadn't meant the unspoken words that this was it for good when he'd walked away. But the caller ID said it was her older sister calling.

"Hey, Rox." Taylor grinned and then held up her six-month-old son to pretend to give his auntie smooches. "What's up—holy cow, sis, you look terrible."

Roxy inspected herself for the first time in a couple days. Bags under her eyes, which were red and puffy from the number of times one of Tag's songs had brought her to tears, or the fact that she'd driven the love of her life away had caught up with her and she'd started sobbing.

"I'm fine. Just doing a lot of introspection."

"About...?" Taylor raised an eyebrow and stashed Tucker in a baby seat next to her, turning her full attention to the phone call.

"Love. How much Tag probably makes and if he can afford a lot of plane tickets. The fact that the romantic part of my brain is maybe broken." She slumped her head down onto the table.

Taylor whistled. "Okay, so. He makes a loooooot of money, that's the one thing I can answer for you. And maybe now was not the best time to talk about what I called to talk about."

Roxy sat back up and waved her hand. "I could use the distraction. And a shower."

"So. How much you love him has finally caught up with you?" Taylor asked in a low voice, frowning, her expression full of so much sympathy it almost made Roxy break down again.

Roxy shook her head, shrugged, and batted those words away too. "Distraction," she insisted, although her voice cracked.

"Well, this is a doozy of one and it could be kinda awkward, so buckle up." Taylor rubbed her lips together and took a deep breath. "Gavin and I want to move back to the ranch. I know we left you to it for a long time and the ranch probably feels like it's yours now, but Dad did leave it to all of us. We're absolutely open to you discussing what you think is fair for the land or something. I don't know, Rox. That place is part of me, too."

Roxy laughed, and it felt good. "I won't make this awkward. It's like when Savannah got married; this ranch is as much yours as it is mine, and I'd never begrudge you that." She smiled and tilted her head. "I couldn't help picturing a row of matching houses after I'd built mine." Her voice cracked. She wanted those matching houses, didn't she?

She maybe wanted Tag more. And having Gavin and Taylor around meant that Taylor could take a bigger role. Bellamy insisted— and was right—that Roxy wasn't needed all the time for the Arrow C and the Ranch House to run smoothly. But maybe having Taylor around would be mentally freeing. Maybe she could drag her feet less about doing what she should have all along.

"Roxy?" Taylor frowned.

"Distraction!" Roxy insisted and waved her hand around, but her voice came out awfully watery.

"Sweetie, there has got to be a way to work this out," Taylor said anyway, and Roxy didn't miss that her sister's eyes shone with empathetic tears. Poor, tender-hearted Taylor.

"Is there?" Roxy huffed and stood up, bringing her phone along with her as she moved to the stove to heat up some canned chicken noodle soup. How pathetic. At least it was the expensive kind if she couldn't have some of Bellamy's. Or even her mom's. She flipped on the stove and turned to grab a pot from her cupboard.

"Of course," Taylor said. "I know you hate the idea of Nashville, but you could handle part of the year out there, couldn't you? For him?"

Roxy flung her hands out. "I think so, yes. But what if I get bitter about having to give up this life? What if I push him to stop singing? Or what if him cutting back makes him unhappy and *he* gets bitter?" She leaned back, putting her hands behind her and slumping.

Taylor laughed. "You are overthinking this. You can't see the future—"

But Roxy's scream cut her off. In her distracted state, she'd put her hand down on the glass-top burner of her stove.

"Rox?" Taylor cried.

"I'm okay. I think. Ow. Ow. Ow." She danced around the kitchen until she got to the sink. She stared down at the already blistering white skin of her hand and gagged. This could definitely be called a distraction. "Thanks for the advice, Taylor. I think I have to go to urgent care."

—————————

ROXY SAT in the exam room, clenching her unburned hand into a fist and wishing that the ibuprofen she'd taken would kick in. She was so stupid. Tag had her in such a fix that she needed to figure something out—and soon.

Her embarrassment intensified when a tap came on the door and Nash's voice said, "How are things today ... Roxy." He glanced down at the chart in his hand, which he must have just picked up from the nurse if he didn't realize he was coming in to see her.

"Hey."

"Hey." He still stared at her, rather than the chart, and scrubbed at the back of his neck. "Looks like you've come down with something?" he said, which she figured wasn't a bad guess considering how awful the glimpse of her face had been when she'd video-chatted with Taylor. Crying in pain as Bellamy drove her into town—for both her hand and Tag—probably hadn't helped the situation.

"Er, no. Burned my hand." She held it up for him.

He frowned. "How did you do that?" His awkwardness dropped, replaced with concern as he sat on the wheeled stool and came toward her.

"Put my hand on a stove."

Nash's eyebrows shot up as he looked from her hand to her face. "That doesn't sound like you."

"It's been a rough few days."

"You're not..." His awkwardness returned and he spun away to pull on some gloves, as though he'd just remembered she was a patient. "About us?" he asked, avoiding her gaze.

"Um, no. I'm sorry." She dropped her voice, upset that she had to have this conversation now, but it hadn't been a full lie when she told Tag that she and Nash were on a break, so this conversation had to come up sometime.

"No." He waved her off and met her gaze again. "You were right."

"It's my fault, though. From years of running away so that I didn't even understand what I was doing myself. I hate myself a little that you got caught up in that." She moved to take his hand and then grimaced.

He looked down at the floor. "I was pretty angry at first. It felt like maybe all along I'd just been a distraction."

"I'm sorry," she said, her voice low. Because maybe he was right and that made her the worst. Worse than Tag Turner dropping into her life and making a mess.

He looked back at her, a smile plastered on his face. "But the more I thought about what you said, the more I realized we were just good friends—perfect friends, really—and we should have just stayed that way."

"Yeah," she nodded, frowning and grateful that he'd accepted everything in stride. So like Nash.

His smile turned more genuine. "So, apology accepted. Unlike you and Tag, we do have to live in the same town, and I'd rather you didn't run away every time you encounter me. It would make treating this injury hard." He paused. "Unless you're not going to be in town for long?"

She sighed. "I guess that's part of the problem. I don't really know."

He reached over and laid a hand on her leg, his expression full of the friendship he'd just spoken of. "In all honesty, you look awful, Rox. Nashville might be what I'd prescribe."

"That's what I was afraid of."

CHAPTER SEVENTEEN

The bar was packed, every table filled, every seat at the bar, and standing room in the back. When the exclusive tickets had gone on sale that morning for this impromptu concert, they'd been sold within ten minutes. At this bar, Beau had come to listen to Tag after seeing a YouTube video of him. The rest, as they both liked to say, had been history. Tonight, they had promised a sneak peek at some of the new songs going on the album and a healthy dose of Taggart Dubois nostalgia.

Tag figured the rough edges to his heart would make for a stunning performance, maybe one of his best yet. But as he sat backstage preparing, he had the urge to just go home, sit in his bedroom, and play his guitar until the hurt went away.

He took a deep breath to channel it. He sang the song he'd started working on the night he came home from Wyoming, humming through the parts he wasn't quite sure on yet. By the time Beau pushed open the door to the small dressing room, he was ready to go.

The fans in the bar went wild when Tag stepped on stage and he grinned at the fact that about seventy-five percent of the audience was female. Maybe dating more seriously than he had in the past would be a good idea. He'd taken women out on a regular basis, but his rigorous schedule and half his heart still belonging to Roxy made relationships difficult. He could still have the family he'd dreamed of having with Roxy, he'd just have to take a slight turn on the path he'd thought he was headed down.

He started out with the promise he'd made to give them a peek at some of the new songs, skipping "Front Porch," as he'd dubbed the newest song he'd written for Roxy, instead singing one with an ode to Bellamy's biscuits in the second verse. The excitement in the room practically jumped up on stage and engulfed him, propelling him through the rest of the song and into an old favorite, one he'd written at just sixteen, that had proven to be his biggest hit to date. He'd sang it enough that usually he could croon lyrics about Roxy without bringing her to mind, but not tonight. Words about the way she smiled and how she didn't know how much he stared at her threatened to choke him. It brought out a raspy quality to his voice that made a few of the women in the audience cry out. When Tag had first gone to Little River, he expected to at least come away with his best music ever, even if he didn't succeed in winning Roxy back. Maybe it was the fact that he'd come so close, closer than he expected, that made this harder than any time since Laramie. Maybe having a daily dose of her was more potent than he'd expected. In any case, things were going to be raw for him for longer, harder to package away as "this will be great for song-writing." He just had to get through it.

He chose some high-energy songs next with standard country-life lyrics, keeping the excitement high while staying away from the hardest memories. On a stage in front of thousands, the emotions churning through him might have been to his advantage, but the intimacy of only a hundred or so fans had caught him off guard.

He couldn't ignore all the requests they shouted at him though, which led to another song from his second album, the one he'd written after Laramie, charged with more pain and clearly a break-up song. He had to get off this stage—and possibly spend a few days holed up at his farm rather than spending another long day at the studio. He'd underestimated what his break-up had done to him and his ability to power through.

"I want to thank you all for coming tonight," he said when he'd finished, and a groan of disappointment echoed through the room. "You all know this place means a great deal to me." The cheers gave way, which was a relief, as the crowd reluctantly accepted the end had come.

"One more!" came a shout from the back that gripped his heart for a second. The voice had sounded like Roxy's, enough to convince him to pack it up as quickly as possible. Hallucinating thanks to a broken heart was a new one for Tag, but he bet it would make for some awesomely painful lyrics.

Others echoed the woman's request, and Tag cast a pleading look at Beau, who sat at the end of the bar nearest to Tag. But his manager wasn't even looking at him, instead he squinted into the darkness of the bar, his expression surprised.

The crowd shouted song requests and Tag took a deep breath, prepared to give a heartfelt apology and get away. Then a voice rang out, the same one who'd started the call for an encore. "How about Roxy's Song?"

He didn't mistake it that time. Didn't hallucinate it. The woman herself stood up from where she sat at a table in the back and one of the lights at the bar caught her across the face. To his knowledge, this was the first time she'd seen him perform in eight years—excepting his impromptu concerts at the ranch.

"Roxy?" He'd stepped away from his mike, but it caught enough of her name that several people in the front row turned, and then the whispers started. "Is that her?" "*The* Roxy?" And then it turned to cries of, "Sing it! Sing it!"

He obliged. How could he not with her in the crowd? He let loose the full weight of his "dreamy" voice, as many a female fan had praised him. He didn't know what she was doing there or why or if it was a good idea to lay his heart out on the line again for her after so many times, but he did. He sang the original lyrics and improvised a few to include her name—earning some whistles and more soft cries of excitement from the crowd. He couldn't tell in the dim lights, but he'd guess his girl blushed more than a few times at the attention on her.

He didn't miss that more than a few people held up cell-phones, recording the song.

When he came to the end, he stepped off the stage and made his way to the back, where she still stood, smiling at him in a way he'd only seen once before—that night in Laramie when she was lost in the song and hadn't thought of rejecting him yet.

He reached her as he strummed the last few lines, but he stopped before the last line, swinging his guitar around his back as he sang it, then pulled her into his arms. "What are you doing here?" He had to lean over next to her ear so she'd hear over the cheering filling the bar.

"Figured it was about time I heard what all the fuss was about." With that, she clapped a hand around his neck and pulled him toward her lips, as though she couldn't wait another second. Tag wrapped his arms around her, lifting her up off her feet as she kissed him, the whooping around him rising and the rapid clicking of phone cameras. It wasn't the desperate, hungry kiss they'd shared on her porch. This one held promise he recognized that he'd missed in the first one. It held the future, and that made him lighter and happier. He laughed against Roxy's lips.

"You thought me singing that song in Little River was bad? This is going to be all over Instagram in a few minutes."

She leaned her forehead to his. "All that matters to me is that one person knows how I feel." She leaned up into him, singing softly to his ear, *"Let me sit with you on our front porch swing. Sing me to sleep every night. Hold our babies; hold me. I've never felt anything more right."*

Tag didn't realize this moment could get any better until he heard his girl's singing voice, sexy and low in his ear. She had sung along back in high school more than a time or two, and he had known she could carry a tune just fine, but she had never sung just to him. It set everything inside him on fire. "Baby, you are speaking my language." He held her tighter.

"'Bout time I learned."

Grabbing her hand, he pulled her backstage, waving and grinning at the fans still cheering and everyone chattering and snapping more pictures. When he had pushed the door shut behind him in the dressing room, he shed his guitar and pulled her back into him, kissing her again and nearly falling into the way she kissed him back —fully, no reservations, no reluctance, no goodbye on the horizon.

"Did I just play my last concert?" he asked when he pulled away.

She shook her head. "No. No, I still can't ask you to do that. But we can meet halfway. If you cut back your schedule, make Little River home instead of that—really pretty—farm here. Maybe you can keep a house here or something that we can stay in when we have to? Or maybe you can keep the farm. I don't know. How rich are you?"

Happiness broke through Tag and he couldn't stop the laughter, full of relief, full of excitement, full of the best yet to come. "Are you serious, Rox? You're going to travel with me?"

She nodded. "When I can. I won't raise babies on the road, Tag." Her expression turned fierce, and he pulled her close again to reassure her. "I'll miss you when you're gone, but we'll make it work. We'll find compromises. It's not worth it not to."

He swept away some hair that had fallen across her face. "I've missed you enough the last eight years to figure out how to manage it knowing I get to come home to you always."

She tilted her head at him, her expression going sad, enough that he leaned over to kiss it and make it go away, but she held onto his face and stopped him. "I'm sorry I didn't believe it was real, for so long. That I let your career stand between us when it didn't need to. Tag, you've written some beautiful words and if I would've just *listened,* I could have saved us both a lot of hurt."

He couldn't help that he cast her a mischievous smile. "I wouldn't be half so famous, darlin'." He didn't give her a chance to laugh at his fake southern drawl before he kissed her again, a past time he found he might write at least half a dozen songs about alone.

"Then I guess you're welcome," she murmured. And before they got lost in another long-awaited kiss, she whispered, "I love you as big as those mountains we call home, mister."

"I love you as big as the stars above them, honey."

EPILOGUE

This sweet little thing had only been alive a few minutes, but Tag already knew he would never get enough of her. Her dark hair had a touch of auburn, like her mama, and just staring at eight pounds, three ounces of adorableness convinced him that his heart must have grown in size to contain so much love for both her and Roxy. He couldn't help the song that welled up in his soul, getting louder and louder with every second the baby's pretty blue eyes stared at him. How could he ever write enough songs to express all the love he felt, to express how blessed he was to have Roxy, to have this precious baby? He could fill a hundred albums alone at the way the baby's tiny fingers wrapped around one of Roxy's.

He reached for the small notebook in his back pocket, but his wife's hand caught his. "Live in the moment for once, Star." She chuckled. She'd said the same thing after they'd said their vows and Tag had to resort to scribbling words onto the napkins at the reception.

So he shifted back to leaning over the bed, his face next to Roxy's as they both admired the most beautiful baby on the planet, no question. Tag tucked away all the words stacking up in his throat, aching to be let loose and let the world know.

"Man, and I thought all that heartbreak you handed me was the diamond mine of lyrics…"

Roxy took her eyes off the blue-eyed beauty lying on her chest long enough to scowl at Tag. "Are you really going to bring that up now?"

He leaned over to kiss her, not bothering to keep the grin from his face. "This moment is ten times sweeter because of what it took to get here," he whispered.

She laughed at him. "Oh, hush with that sweet talk. We both know you wouldn't have minded me figuring things out several years earlier."

"Nah, Rox, we both had some learning to do." He'd pondered many a time how the pain of being apart from her had allowed him to understand how crazy amazing the joy of being together could be. He rested his head against Roxy's again, still staring down at his baby girl. His. The smile hadn't let up since she'd arrived. Heck, he'd had a hard time shaking it since the day Roxy told him.

He didn't realize he'd started humming until Roxy laughed. "Go on, let it out," she said, her own grin spreading. "Grab your ukulele if you have to," she teased. He'd used it several times during the long labor to help Roxy through it.

"You know you want me to." He reached back and took it from behind the chair and strummed a little, still humming as he let the words come together. When he started singing, Lola's eyes drooped shut and she gave a sweet baby sigh of sleep.

"Mmmm, just like her mama," Tag sang softly. That line would certainly make the cut, even if he was teasing now.

"It's a weakness." Roxy nestled a cheek against the top of Lola's head, closing her eyes as she turned toward Tag and hummed along. More than a few nurses took their time crossing by their doorway, much like the ones he'd caught hovering there when he'd played for Roxy during labor. "This is going to be your best yet." Roxy reached over to cup his cheek and smile sleepily at him.

He quit playing to lean over her. "You always say that."

"And I'm always right."
"That's why I love you," he hummed.
"Big as the mountains."
"Big as the stars."

Look for more *Love in Little River* stories coming soon!

In the meantime, sign up for the Raneé S. Clark newsletter for the latest releases: http://bit.ly/rscnews.

You can find more contemporary romance from Raneé at: http://bit.ly/rscama.

ABOUT THE AUTHOR

Raneé S. Clark is the author of five contemporary romances and one historical novel, *Beneath the Bellemont Sky*. When she's not writing, she's reading lovely romances, buying too many clothes, chauffeuring three boys to football, basketball, soccer, and piano, and praying that her husband survives his latest outdoor adventure.

You can find out more about Raneé's writing on Facebook and Instagram.